MW00830671

HUMANS WANTED

Humans Wanted

Copyright © 2017 Cuppatea Publications

All rights reserved. No part of this book may be repro-
duced or transmitted in any form or by any electronic or
mechanical means, including photocopying, recording or
by any information storage and retrieval system, without
the express written permission of the copyright holder,
except where permitted by law. This collection is a work
of fiction. Names, characters, places and incidents are
either the product of the author's imagination, or, if real,
used fictitiously.

ISBN-13: 978-0692900031
ISBN-10: 0692900039

Book Design by Nuance Interactive
Cover Design by Owl Quest Creative
Cover Images from Shutterstock
Published by Cuppatea Publications
Denver, CO

Printed in the USA

ACKNOWLEDGEMENTS

Many thanks go to Iztarshi for giving me permission to use their post for this anthology. More thanks go to the backers who made this a reality (and who are listed after the stories with our thanks). And thank you, reader. You are wanted.

CONTENTS

WHAT MAKES US HUMAN?

Humans are tough. Humans can last days without food. Humans heal so quickly, they pierce holes in themselves or inject ink under their epidermis for fun. Humans will walk for days on broken bones in order to make it to safety. Humans will literally cut off bits of themselves if trapped by a disaster.

You would be amazed what humans will do to survive. Or to ensure the survival of others they feel responsible for.

That's the other thing. Humans pack-bond, and they spill their pack-bonding instincts everywhere. Sure it's weird when they talk sympathetically to broken spaceships or try to pet every lifeform that scans as non-toxic. It's even a little weird that just existing in the same place as them for long enough seems to make them care about you.

But if you're hurt, if you're trapped, if you need someone to fetch help? You really want a human.

When Iztarshi's Tumblr post first came across my dash, the thing that made me so excited about the concept was that it showed humanity in a light that was not only positive in science fiction, but also useful. It was unusual to see human qualities presented as positive in a world where we so often like to condemn our faults and ignore our triumphs. When our good traits are mentioned, we get very excited about when presented with the opportunity to explore that and the inspiration to do so.

When I shared the post, it exploded with comments from my fellow authors about the stories they'd write. It showed me that there was not only a need for these sort of stories, but a burning desire to express them.

So often in science fiction, humans are seen as the least favorable members of galactic society. Humans are the base species from which all the other aliens can be compared to. Aliens are more culturally developed, they are better able to handle extreme planetary atmospheres, more scientifically advanced, or more cognitively capable. Humans are only good for cannon fodder or seen as a blight for reproducing so quickly. Very rarely do we see science fiction with aliens that view humans as a species in a particularly favorable light.

For the most part we are seen as the trash species of the galaxy, the ones most likely to ruin everything. In some cases, humans are somewhat useful, but for the most part they are either independent or an inconvenience. It is rare to see science fiction in which humans are viewed as contributing members of interplanetary society.

This is a shame because humans, despite our faults, are wonderful. We are ingenious, creative, caring, persistent. We fight for what we believe in with a ferocity that transcends reason and have hearts that are capable of so much love that they can break from its lack.

When I was reading submissions for this anthology, I searched for the stories that most embodied the heart of the original prompt. These twelve stories show not only who we are, but who we could be. They speak of the human experience from a human point of view and also show us from an alien point of view. The tales give a template of our future, and the relationships we can forge in a galactic civilization that might just welcome us.

These stories span the breadth of the universe where humans do more than fight in wars and die in pointless battles. In this anthology, humans travel to the edge of the galaxy and through their unique nature, inspire those with whom they come into contact.

Some of these stories show humans as helpers, others as rescuers. The humans in these stories are clever, brave, determined, and above all, human. Their compassion transcends what we would normally expect of ourselves and shows the entire universe what we can be. They visit worlds and places beyond our wildest imaginations and yet they still bring parts of humanity with them to remind us who we are.

It is significant that many of these stories are written from alien points of view. Writing truly alien perspectives, ones that share nothing with the human experience, has often been recognized as difficult, if not entirely impossible. Each of the species in these stories shows us how we view our pride, our despair, our wonder through an alien lens and through that lens, we can see ourselves as we are and as we can be.

We are better than we think we are.

We are wanted.

SIDEKICK

Jody Lynn Nye

Tinis huddled in the smallest possible bundle underneath the moving ramp, trying to pick out the sounds of her kidnappers' footfalls among the other myriad noises. All the sensations of the outer world hammered like a whirlwind of pins and spikes. She hurt so much she had to force herself not to cry out in pain. Everything that touched her seemed to be trying to steal some of her energy. She had to conserve all her strength, not let it be expended in terror. She was a very young child a long, long way from home. Where were Mo and Ro and Ga?

The place where the evil ones had held her for three day-cycles smelled of meadows and dreams, a sure sign that drugs had been floated on the air. Her pale blue skin still tingled where the tiny, aerosolized droplets had settled. She did not yet understand chemistry, but she understood durations. Its evaporation should have resulted in continued efficacy at preventing ultraviolet light from striking her skin and reenergizing her system, but it did not.

She forced herself to remain conscious while the evil ones' guard went away from its post for recharging. It was a similar mechanical protector to the kind her family used. Tinis knew how long their systems could go without intense bombardment of proton particles, because sometimes her own caretaker had to undertake energy restoration in the way she needed to feed. She had waited until the mid-darkness, when the nourishing ultraviolet light had been turned off and the evil ones were certain she had fallen asleep. As soon as she sensed the protector's stores lowering to suboptimum levels, it had withdrawn. The metacharge would not take long.

Tinis had seized her opportunity, and fled, leaving the petals of the borrowed sleepflower tucked securely around the cushiony pad at its center, as if she still lay there. She took nothing with her but the white smock and soft booties she had been wearing when abducted.

Outside the chamber where she had been held, she recognized nothing. Other sleepflowers bloomed in rooms around the center stem of the building, meaning that more Ocetians lived here; whether prisoners or not, she couldn't tell. During her incarceration, she had not sensed anything beyond the walls of her room. Everything was densely shielded, blocking her abilities. When she had emerged into the open air, sensation slammed into her like a physical force. She had run, desperate for peace from the thrumming of life forms and machinery, and violent, selfish thought. Her slim, almost scrawny body, had been easy to conceal in between the ribs of the homeflower, but now she was at the mercy of the outside world. Her prison had also been the only respite for lengths in any direction. The travel ramp under which she had eventually sheltered let out a soothing harmonic above its heavy rumble, dampening the frightening noises somewhat.

Feeding intruded upon her thoughts now. Since her escape, she had absorbed a little of the ultraviolet light from the blue sun that Ocet circled, which restored her mental faculties. Now she needed sustenance to support her bodily functions. She concentrated, sending her sensing mind out to the farthest distance she could reach. Nowhere could she smell the violet sunberries that she and her kind needed to live. They had plenty—oh, so succulent!—in the confines where she had been held. Sunberries tasted of syrupy, spicy warmth, like an embrace from Mo or Ga, but she wouldn't return to that place.

Her senses touched many unsuitable foodstuffs, the kind favored by the many visitors to Ocet, as well as the visitors themselves. Three different races had come a few year-turns ago to trade for sunberries and whatever the Ocetia could offer. Ro said often, when xi thought Tinis wasn't listening, that they had worn out their welcome. Their cultures had changed Ocet, and not all for good.

The numbers of alien strangers in the city over-whelmed her with their strange thoughts and jarring energies. She drew her sensing mind back to her with a snap, and curled in on herself, wrapping her four delicate arms around her two thin knees. Slender, yellow-skinned Pidirians, with their sharp minds intruding into every-thing, went here and there in their fast-moving personal sleds like living lightning bolts. Ocetians avoided them but for formal occasions when their energy was muted by societal agreement. Various-tinted Humans, big and slow-moving, ambled along. Ocetians felt as though they were big children, wondering at everything they saw. Hot, red Ne'ru'bu seemed angry at everything. Their thoughts burned her when she touched one of them.

At her age, she would not normally have been acquainted with any of these. The shielding in her family's domicile protected the delicate young within from any outward energy emissions. She wouldn't have gone abroad unless she was in a transport capsule. She had had many visitors, though, once Ga learned, quite by accident, that Tinis could detect the presence of even trace amounts of horom, a rare and precious mineral. Ga had been excited because that sensitivity meant Tinis could hope to become a transporter, one who connected points of space to one another. Her mental abilities homed in on those tiny particles of the transuranic element and caused a chain reaction that resulted in instantaneous transference.

He sought out investors who might sponsor Tinis's training, meaning their humble home hosted numerous wealthy Ocetia families as well as some strangers. Ga trotted her out in late evening hours, when she would rather be tucked into her sleepflower, and the adults engaged in deep discussions over her head, both literally and figuratively.

Screech! Thud thud thud! Tinis cowered as noise erupted above her. Two—no, three—personal conveyances had attempted to move into the same lane at the same time. By the whining, one of the capsules had been too damaged to move. Pieces from the conveyances tumbled down over the edge of the roadway and scattered on the clay near Tinis. Arguing in more than one language boomed out. She felt the anger of a Ne'ru'bu, strained words from more than one Ocetian, and slow rumbling from a Human. The shouting stopped as another Ocetian joined them, probably a Peacemaker. Tinis wanted to reach out to xir to help her get home. Tinis crept partway from her hiding place, waiting. After a long time, the Peacemaker had xir information and insisted the others move on. Tinis's energy sagged. She was getting so hungry, but she feared the evil ones would come back.

"Hello," a voice came from above, startling her back into her crevice. A Human peered down at her. "Don't run."

He—Humans were always 'he' to the Ocetians; it was so difficult to tell their many genders apart—had jumped down from the moving path to gather up pieces from the wreck. He hunkered down to look beneath the path. She blinked at him. He was huge, much bigger than Ga, clad in dark green, like a healthy plant, with bronze-colored skin and fleshy protuberances that ran horizontally above his eyes, down the middle of his face and around the edge of his mandible, and coarse black fuzz on the top of his head. They were so unlike Ocetians, who were hairless, with smooth, almost spherical heads. "Are you hungry?"

His Ocetian language was terrible, so bad that she could only understand him by prying into his emotions to sense his concern. Humans responded to head bobs, so she nodded. He pulled on his back and a portion of it came away with an alarming tearing noise—no, that was the kind of container they often bore to contain personal goods. From the cloth bag, he brought out two brightly colored commercial packets and offered them to her. She wouldn't put out any of her hands to a stranger. He sensed that, and put them on the ground instead. Tinis hesitated until he backed away, then reached for the little bags.

The first contained a heavy protein concentrate, unsuitable for young like her. She pushed it away. The other—oh, relief! —contained sunberries. She tore it open and poured the round purple nodules into her hand. They were dried and covered in sucrose powder, rendering them into candy. Humans liked things very sweet. Tinis gulped down three, and immediately felt better. The syrupy sweetness spread throughout her mouth and down her throat. She could almost trace the improvement as her skin regained its tone and natural defenses against outward impediment, and her body stopped fighting against her mind. She put the bag on the ground and poked it toward the Human with a tentative foot.

"Don't you want more than that?" he asked. The Human seemed puzzled that she rejected the first envelope and left the second almost full, but how could such a primitive understand their superior metabolism? She had eaten what she needed for restoration.

"Thank you for your kindness," she said, rising to her feet. She steadied herself with one set of arms and brushed her light garment with the other. "I must go home now."

"You're just a child," he said, and his internal senses broadcast protective worry. "I should accompany *you*."

Tinis straightened herself. "That will not be necessary. I can get home."

But how? She was so far away she couldn't sense any of her loved ones. She glanced over the edge of the roadway. Broken pieces of the carry-capsules lay strewn in heaps. No stop for public conveyances was close by. She would have to walk until a kind stranger halted.

"All right," he said. "Then maybe you can help me. My taxi got broken up in the accident, and I don't have any way to get to where I'm going, or where I'm supposed to go. All those others left me here by myself."

Tinis opened one small palm. "The Peacemaker should have helped you. Xi was asking if you needed assistance."

The Human frowned. "Is that what she was saying?" He sighed and sat down on a chunk of broken capsule. "This place gets me all confused. I'm supposed to visit a family on the far edge of town, but it isn't a town at all the way I know places. And there's no edges. You live in flowers, and they're scattered all over the map, not in any kind of order I can see."

He prattled on. Tinis didn't understand all his words, but she was willing to help him. "Do you know the shape of the flower you seek?" she asked. "Our homes call to us in shape, scent and size, not lines as in your world."

His lumpy face crinkled as he thought.

"Six petals," he said promptly, and drew upon the air with his hands. "Blue. They have pointy tips that touch up at the top of the blossom. It's kind of pretty."

Tinis closed her eyes to think. "My home has six petals like that one, so you need to look among ones that stand twelve to fifteen heights high, perhaps in the meadow where mine lies."

She gulped, but felt she had to be brave for this helpless Human. "Come with me. We will find your friends."

"Maybe we can ask your progenitors how to find my destination," the Human said, looking skeptical.

"Why? I can read flower-heights as well as they. Better than Ro."

The fleshy mouth spread sideways, and the square white bones set in its jaw appeared. "Who's Ro?"

"What are you called?" Tinis asked, not comfortable discussing family with a Human.

"Rish," he said. "It's short for a much longer name that I don't like. What do they call you?"

"M'Tinis'desim Oghal Yuirimha," she said, with a mischievous glance. "When I am older and have gained accomplishments it will be longer still." Rish looked dismayed at having to form all those syllables. "But you may say 'Tinis.' That is my use-name."

"Thanks!" he said, gusting a breath out. His breathing vent, unlike a good Ocetian, had a strip of flesh that bifurcated the opening at the bottom, so the air divided and went in two directions. "Now, if you'll just help me get where I'm going, Lady Tinis, I'll be very grateful."

He looked around, nervously peering at the short, pale-lilac homeflowers close by and the capsules buzzing past them on the moving roadway. Humans were even more foolish than she thought they would be. How could a grown being get lost so easily? He seemed afraid of not knowing where he was. How was it that her small kind could identify such subtle points, and big people like Humans and Ne'ru'bu could so easily get lost?

"I will protect you," she said, reaching up to take his big, rough hand in both of her right ones.

"Thanks!" he said again, squeezing her long fingers gently. "I'll be your sidekick."

"What does that mean?" Tinis asked, trying out the harsh syllables on her tongue.

"Oh, well, a sidekick's job is to keep the hero amused, carry the bags, and express admiration when the hero does something very clever and saves the day."

Tinis's eyes widened. "I did not know there were such things. I would enjoy having a...sidekick. Tell me a story of your people."

Rish was all too happy to talk as he loped beside her small, mincing steps. "Well, we Humans are pretty new to interstellar relations. We've been trying to find inhabited stars for more than a century, so you can understand how exciting it was to find so many different species of intelligent life in such a small area of space, not that space is small...."

Shutting out his voice, Tinis reached out with all her senses, feeling toward home and the minute trace of horom that Ga kept to demonstrate her talents to visitors. One of the families who had come to discuss her services had gifted Tinis with a particle of her own, scarcely more than a molecule. It was embedded in the identification bangle on her wrist. She wished sincerely that both portions were large enough to move matter at that distance, and that she had had the training to join them and make the transit in a twinkling. Still, the two fragments of mineral spoke to each other. She could follow the vector and find her way home.

Once she had fixed upon the point, it was easy to keep it in the forefront of her mind. With sufficient ultra-violet rays beaming down upon her from the blue sun, she would never lose contact. They walked in between the massive stalks of colorful homeflowers and sandy green shrubclusters, with Rish remarking upon things that were different than on his homeworld.

Just to amuse herself, Tinis reached out another tendril of her senses, feeling for more horom elsewhere. It was so rare, only one or two homes had any within them. A few bits of it were on the move, a couple on ships transiting to distant worlds or space stations, and others being taken from one place to another, there on Ocet. She touched numerous busy minds surrounding the few traces within the meadow valley, where the universities and training centers grew in shrubclusters. Tinis was proud to think she would be in one of those someday, learning to be a navigator and creating those transitions herself.

She felt sad that the families who had come to visit their home had not all been interested in sponsoring her education. They were wealthy enough, Mo said so. They all checked her ID bracelet, to be certain that Tinis was entitled to the Oghal lineage she claimed. They surveyed her intelligence assessment, health records, images of her at play, and watched her pass tests of horom detection with one hundred percent accuracy. Under the guidance of instructors from the Ocet Grand University, she had actually moved an object from their facility to her home by joining the two vibrations, proving her natural aptitude. All the families had been impressed. A number wanted to think about the proposition. A few went away, broadcasting the attitude of dismissal.

One...one family bothered Tinis. Even Ga, who had always been ambitious for the offspring's success, had noticed. The Sughul clan paid no attention to the rest of her qualifications, only scrutinizing the search results. They put a question to her parents: would the Oghal clan be willing to consider Tinis as a spotter to horom mining? The mineral was depressingly difficult to find, making it expensive far out of proportion to its rarity. Spotters would make the search far more cost effective. She would be well-paid. Ga, horrified, had disabused them of the notion. Tinis had the talent for navigation. She wouldn't work as a lowly miner. The Sughul family had withdrawn, but not before making two more attempts to convince Ga to let them take Tinis.

She had too much time to think while they walked in the direction of the family flower. Something in the evil place where she had been held reminded her of the Sughul family. The taint seemed to have followed her to the place where she had been hiding when Rish found her. She even felt a sense of it coming from him. She looked up at the Human. He caught her glimpse and stared down at her, showing small, white mouth bones in the Human way. She sensed no malice in him, but could he be an unwitting pawn of the Sughul family?

"We should go toward the main road," Tinis said, suddenly wanting the trek over swiftly. "We can find a waiting point for public capsules and hire one to take me to my home."

He squinched his lumpy face.

"Do you have money? Will they take your ID for transport?"

She looked down at the thin white bangle and sighed. "No. But if we explain it is an emergency, they will notify the nearest Peacemaker."

"I'm afraid of more accidents," Rish said, dropping his voice to a murmur. "Besides, my credit globe was smashed in the accident. So was my communicator. I'll have to ask my friends to help me get a replacement." He held out a handful of blue glass shards. The lumps on his face spread farther apart in concern. "Without them, I have no ID. I could get in trouble being out here without documents. Your governing families don't like unidentified aliens wandering around. Please help me."

Tinis felt sorry for him. He was so unprepared for being far away from home, much more than she was. She took his hand again. "Then we will walk."

They plodded on, in between the stems, treading the dark red grass and the sweet-smelling purple blooms that grew among it, stepping carefully over rocks to avoid the venomous millipedes that often hid beneath them. She had never been so far from home before. Her estimate that it would take fifteen time-measures to reach home began to seem too optimistic.

The sun reached noon height. From the loud pouch on Rish's back, he produced a strange round hat with a protruding bill that shielded his eyes, and a folded cloth of soft, spice-scented white fabric that he tied over her head. It formed a little flap that shaded her face.

"I think you're getting too much sun," he said. "Do you need a couple more berries? Some water? Do you need to rest?"

"Not yet," she said. She had been shocked that he would touch her without permission, but the cloth was a comfort. How kind of him to think of it. She rubbed a fold of it between her fingers. It felt...well loved.

She scanned the meadow and the secondary lanes that crisscrossed it. To keep Rish from being detected by the authorities, they should take as few roadways as possible and stay away from shrubclusters that might have sentry beasts. She pointed to a gap in between two stems through which she could see bright violet garden blossoms. "Let us go that way."

The tall wild grass gave way to a carpet of white lichens. Blooms of every color had been arranged in undulating beds along the edge. She glanced up at the bright yellow homeflower above them, wondering if she could beg the inhabitants to notify her family and save them the rest of their hike. But the scent of evil still haunted her. She didn't know whom she could trust, and that included Rish. She wished she had studied Humans more.

Rustling in the flowerbeds drew her attention. She caught her breath as a brown millipede, almost as long as she was, erupted from among the bushes. Tinis froze, terrified. The beast made straight for her, its sharp mandibles clattering.

"Run!" Rish said. "Now!"

She dithered for a moment, torn as to which way to flee. The Human picked her up with one hand and tossed her effortlessly up against the stem of the house. She caught the thick stalk with all four arms and did her best to hang on. From a pocket deep inside his green tunic, Rish drew a silver wand and fired off a blossom of red. The burst enveloped the millipede's body. The gigantic crawler tossed its head and kept moving toward Tinis's perch. Rish's dark eyes widened, showing white circles around their center. "*Mama padrona!*" He fired again. The burst burned two of its legs and one bulbous eye. It let out a fierce hiss and swished its forked tail.

Tinis cowered. Such beasts came in from the wilderlands occasionally, hiding in undergrowth. Every homeflower had modern systems installed to protect them against the millipedes and other dangers, but they were inside, not outside. They hunted their prey remorselessly and tore it to pieces. Their bite was poisonous—Rish probably didn't know that!

"Don't let it bite you!" she screamed.

"I won't," he called back, not taking his eyes off the creature. He didn't sound as frightened as she thought he should be. He dodged back and forth, as the millipede's head swiveled on its top body segment. It lunged at him. He evaded it with more dexterity than she believed a Human could show, then stepped forward on one foot. She gasped. The creature went for his leg. He brought the other foot over and onto the back of its head, then crushed downward. The body went insane, thrashing and clawing at him with all its sharp feet. Rish ignored the snags and tears to his green trousers, as he fired the wand again and again, until the body sagged to the ground.

When he was certain the twitching creature was dead, Rish left it and went to hold out his arms to Tinis. She dropped into them and examined his face with concern.

"You let it scratch you," she said, almost accusingly.

"Well, you told me not to let it bite me," he said. "I guessed you had a reason not to warn me about the claws. Was I wrong?"

"No...no! You are smarter than I thought you were. I hope you are not hurt too badly."

He showed his mouth bones again.

"Thanks, little one. It's just a few grazes. I can mend

the pants when I get to my friends' house. Let's go on. Hope we don't meet any more of those."

Instead of putting her down, he held her cradled in one of his big arms and let her direct his path. The ride was a novelty. Humans were far more sturdily built than Ocetians. Even Ro had not carried her around like that since she was very small. She had to admit that it felt very comforting.

When they had to cross roadways, she directed Rish behind bushes and stalks to hide him from passing capsules and other pedestrians. He pulled leafy branches around to conceal the two of them from view. His caution at being caught out without identification meant they had to go out of their way again and again. Always, her link to the horom meant she knew how to point toward her home. Soon, they would be close enough that she would be able to sense her family, and they her. They must be so worried!

Every so often, Rish offered her a sunberry or two and a sip of pure water from a clear, flexible sack. His long strides fell into a rhythm that lulled her. He only spoke if she asked him a question or if he needed to be reassured of their vector. In the heat and the softness, she drowsed off to sleep.

"*Merda!*"

The sharp exclamation awoke her. The sun was at a much more acute angle than it had been. Tinis raised her large eyes to Rish's face. He had a device in his hand, like a primitive communicator. When he saw her looking at him, he snapped it closed and shoved it into the pack on his back.

"What is that?"

"A tracker," he said.

"What are you tracking?" she asked, suddenly alarmed. "I thought you didn't know where you were going?"

"It's not a where-tracker," he said. "It's a

who-tracker."

"Your friends?" she asked.

"Not exactly." He clutched her a little closer. The force of his embrace made her squeak a protest. He opened his arm slightly, and patted her on the head. "Sorry. We have to run. Keep me on beam, Lady Tinis."

"I'm afraid!" she cried. "Who are you, Rish?"

"Your friend," he said. "I will never harm you. Trust me just a little while, all right?"

She had no real choice. He was so much stronger than she was that he could break her bones the way he had smashed the head of the millipede.

He veered around the edge of a huge dusty-green shrubcluster. Ululations sounded behind them. She feared guardbeasts. The gray-scaled insectoids were large enough to eat a youngster her size. Rish must have understood that meant peril. He dashed up the nearest slope and over a rise, plunging them into the thicket of untamed undergrowth along a narrow track that must have been a beast-trail. Tinis ducked down to spare her thin skin from the thorns that lashed out at them.

More sounds came from behind them, and voices. She could not pick out any words. They weren't the angry tones of a Ne'ru'bu or the quick burr of a Piridian voice, but Ocetians. To her horror, she realized that she recognized one voice. He had been in the evil place. He was one of her captors! There was something else about him that troubled her. An attractive hum that sounded in her mind made her realize he had a fragment of horom in his possession. It would respond to the one on her person, a reaction perceptible even to those who were incapable of uniting their emanations. Terrified, she nestled into Rish's arm.

"That way," she said, as he hesitated at a fork in the rough-trodden path. Rish turned at her direction.

Rapid, rhythmic pounding came from inside his torso. She didn't sense fear in him, but resolution.

Branches and leaves slapped at them as Rish ran, leaping over the roots of home flowers and ducking down into hollows.

"How many are there?" he asked her.

"Three and a protector," she said, at once. "They are angry—how do you know I can sense them?"

He smiled. "You're pretty special, Lady Tinis," he said. "Let's go."

Running in the shade with the sun beginning to go down, her mental faculties began to blur. She snatched the cloth from her head to let the fading beams strike her pale blue skin. The ultraviolet restored her. At the edge of her sensing abilities, she felt the comfortable aura of her homeflower. She wrapped all four arms around herself as her mind regained its acuity.

Rish had a tracker that told him they were being followed, but how was it the Ocetians behind her came to be following *them*? Was he pretending to be afraid? She delved into his emotions with all her senses, desperate to believe in him. He had shown so many talents and abilities that she had never suspected. Was subterfuge among them?

"You know, that tickles," Rish said, without looking down at her. "It makes me itch behind my eyes and inside my ears. Why not just ask me what you want to know?"

"I...I'm sorry," she said. "It is rude to intrude on another sentient being's thoughts."

"It's okay. I wish I could do that sometimes."

"Are you truly afraid of the people behind us?" Tinis asked.

"Yes," Rish said grimly. "I really am."

Tinis.

Mo? Tinis almost cried out in relief. The warmth of her parent's mental voice enveloped her.

Oh, my child! Where are you? Come home!

I am coming! Find me!

"What is it?" Rish asked, leaping over a jagged rock

and bounding up a slope. He had reached the heath
adjacent to the park only a hundred lengths or so from
her homeflower.

They were runnning in the open now. She looked over
his shoulder. Three Ocetians hurtled out of the undergrowth in pursuit on foot, followed by the domestic robot
which had guarded her in the evil place. They looked and
felt very tired, much less than the Human carrying her. If
he could outpace them for just another quarter measure,
Mo would feel where she was and send Ro and Ga and
some of her cousins to their assistance.

Suddenly, she spotted the rounded lavender petals
of her homeflower peeking up above the surrounding
undergrowth. Her longing to be back home and safe
made her throat tighten.

"There it is," she said, pointing. Rish nodded and
turned toward it. The pounding in his torso grew more
urgent.

One last obstacle remained: the big main road that
wound among the homeflowers in their cluster. She and
Rish had to cross it, and that meant being out in the open
where Rish could be seen. To her horror, the Ocetians
brandished weapons that radiated dangerous energy
signatures, and the protector had a spray like the one
that had been used on her in the evil place to sedate her.

"Are they your enemies?" she asked.

"Now that you mention it, yes," Rish said, his mouth
bones set together grimly. "Hang on, Lady Tinis."

"My family is coming," she said. "They will protect
you."

Almost as soon as she said it, the bushes at the top
of the slope parted, and the family travel capsule hurtled
toward them. The side hatch opened up, and Ro came
out of it running. Xir eyes were wide with horror, but xi
brandished a cultivation rod xi must have picked up from
the garden on xir way out of the homeflower in one of
xir left hands. Five, six, seven more steps, and Rish came

abreast of Tinis's progenitor.

"Take her," Rish said, thrusting Tinis toward Ro. "Get out of here!"

"Thank you," xi said in Human. Rish turned and dropped to one knee, aiming his wand weapon at the oncoming trio.

"Rish! Help him!" Tinis screamed over Ro's shoulder, but her parent ran to the open capsule, tucked xir child into the waiting arms of her three elder cousins, and tapped Ga on the wrist. The capsule shut and rolled back up the hill. The bushes closed behind it, shutting off Tinis's view of Rish just as red energy bolts began to fly. "Help him!"

"No. You are our concern."

The capsule buzzed rapidly over the surface of the road and plunged down the other side of the rise toward the roots of their homeflower. As soon as the conveyance stopped, Ga kicked open the hatch. Tinis's cousins bundled her into the stalk and urged her up the ladder to the main chamber. Mo was waiting, wearing the white worry-robe of a parent in crisis, and enveloped the offspring in her arms. Tinis enjoyed the embrace, feeling safe again among family.

"Child, your return is more than opportune," the delicate progenitor said. She gestured with the upper of her left hands. Tinis looked up to see several visitors sitting on the cushions of honor. "The Sughul clan heard of your disappearance, and came to offer their sorrow."

Tinis fought free of the embrace.

"You honor us with your presence," she said, hastily sketching the correct bow with all four arms. "Mo, I must use the horom."

"Child, no demonstration is necessary," her parent said, with an expression of concern on her smooth face. "Our visitors have already indicated they believe in your talent."

"It is not a demonstration!"

Ro seemed surprised by her youngest child's insistence, but pointed toward one of the storage buds along the wall. Tinis's senses had already told her where it was. She tore open the crisp folds and took the glowing golden crystal from within it. It warmed in her hands, awakening a kind of kinship within her, as though tying her to something infinite that she longed to touch. Tinis couldn't stop to enjoy it, not then.

She felt outside for the horom that the enemy was carrying, and concentrated deeply on joining the emanations. With all the energy in her body, she willed them to unite, bringing the distant fragment to the one in her hands.

Suddenly, the serene room erupted as the protector robot and two of the enemy appeared in their midst. The shell of the protector pressed against Tinis's crystal, proving that it was inside it. Tinis jumped back as the invasion tripped the homeflower's internal protection system. Deafening whoops sounded, shaking the main blossom. A harsh yellow beam lanced out of the ceiling, immobilizing the mechanical. Showers of sleep pollen showered down on the two adult Ocetians. They fell to the floor.

Pounding came from below the main chamber. Ga pursed his thin mouth in amusement.

"Another visitor," he said.

Tinis held herself tense until Rish, smeared with bright red liquid but looking triumphant, dragged the third of the Ocetians up the ladder and into the room. Ro hurried to wind her arms protectively around Tinis. Rish threw the Ocetian, who was bleeding blue from several wounds, onto the floor with his cohorts.

"Greetings," Rish said, showing all his flat white mouth bones. "I see you have your child back. I'd like you to meet the ones responsible for her abduction."

"As the crisis is over, we had best depart," the head of the Sughul clan said, rising hastily.

Rish moved between them and the top of the ladder, holding his big arms so none of them could retreat through the exit.

"Why don't you wait until the Peacemakers get here?" he said,

"What are you doing, Human?" xi asked. "This is a violation of hospitality!"

The lumps of Rish's fleshy face rose toward his fuzzy hair. "How much more of a violation is it to arrange for the kidnapping of a talented child?" he asked.

A squad of Peacemakers in dark red uniforms arrived short time-measures after the homeflower's alarm went off. A solemn-faced officer scanned the inoperative protector and removed the horom crystal, checking its identification markings against one purchased by an employee of the Sughul family. The clan sat silently as the three pursuers and their protector robot were bound and escorted from the homeflower, then it was their turn to be removed from the Oghal household. Tinis still could not take in all that was happening.

Ga plied them all with glasses of nectar and bowls of fresh sunberries. The cousins and siblings hurried around to clean up the traces of the immobilizing powders. Mo came to squeeze Rish's big hands in xir small, delicate ones. Xi looked up at him with as much admiration as an Ocetian would offer to a Human.

"There are not words to thank you enough for restoring our Tinis to us. You found her long before we thought you could. You are everything your advertisement said you were."

Rish's deeply toned skin took on hues of red. Ro fussed about him, dabbing at his face with a clean cloth to remove the traces of battle. He had to bend down so she could reach it. He seemed to take up most of the space in the homeflower's cozy, round gathering room.

"I understand," Rish said. "I'm a mother myself. I just followed the clues you gave. When you said that the Sughuls didn't like you telling them no to their plans, I checked all the places where records said the clan had an interest. I found the domicile where they'd been holding her, but I was too late to pick her up there." He shot Tinis an admiring look. "She was resourceful enough to get out of there herself. They were on her trail when I crashed their capsule."

Tinis looked from one adult to another as they conferred with the Peacemakers. She couldn't believe that her big, foolish Human friend knew her parents. Her senses told her that they did not know him well, but they trusted him absolutely.

"You did that on purpose!" Tinis said, astonished. "And you broke your ID and communicator deliberately?

"I had to make it plausible enough that you would believe in me, Lady Tinis," he said, with a little bow. "I knew you'd be able to read it if I was lying to you. I'm new on this planet. I still needed you to guide me and tip me off as to the dangers on our way here, and you did.... I hope you aren't disappointed that I'm not as dumb as you thought."

Tinis thought about that. She had had time to absorb not only the facts and sensations, but much more of the ultraviolet light that fed her higher centers.

"No," she said at last, trying to emulate his strange smile. "I am pleased. Humans are more than I thought they would be."

He laughed. "And you're pretty special, too, Lady Tinis. Few Human children your age would be as brave and calm as you were."

"Thank you so much for bringing her home safely," Ro said, squeezing Rish's arm in his torn sleeve. "We owe you much more than your fee."

"Oh, she did all the work," Rish said, showing his

mouth bones. He closed one of his eyes at Tinis. She understood it as a mark of friendly conspiracy. "No, I was just along for the ride."

Tinis repeated the expression, to the Human's clear delight.

"Yes," she said. "He is an excellent sidekick."

WWHD: WHAT WOULD HUMANS DO

J. A. Campbell

"We all got the directive. We all know what is in store for us. If we don't submit, we die. If we submit, we'll probably still die. We have to evacuate!" The Kraz Speaker put up their hands in a pleading gesture. "Just because we live deep within a gas giant, doesn't mean our people won't be impacted. The Conquerors have the ability to colonize any type of world."

Raan harrumphed. They'd been talking in circles for over a standard hour now and he was tired of the others' dithering. It was time to announce the first part of the plan to deal with the Conquerors.

"There is a way," he said.

Though the other Speakers were near panic, they all calmed and looked toward Raan. His species always settled the debates between the others, so they would listen.

"The Acamarian Speaker is recognized," Tiff the Acamarian arbitrator said.

"Thank you." Raan stepped onto the circular platform which would amplify his voice to all present in the meeting chamber. Each of the four species had several representatives present to discuss the coming invasion of their home system. "You all know my species was forced from our home system by the Conquerors ages ago. We were unable to repel them. Many of our people died—slaughtered by the millions—we were forced to flee, to rebuild here. There is no way for us to stand against them now. The only species to ever successfully repel the Conquerors is Humans."

This caused a stir, as Raan had intended.

"But Humans are extinct, what good does that do us?" someone shouted from the back. Probably one of the Bihamie, by the gravely voice.

Raan raised his voice. "They are not extinct, merely rare. We have some time before the Conquerors reach us. What we must do is find a Human and discover how they defeated the Conquerors. Then we will be able to stand against the invasion and keep our homes."

It took a moment for his plan to sink in, then many in the room gave their species' equivalent of a cheer.

Raan put up his hands for quiet and allowed himself a quick smile before continuing. "You will each choose one of your finest Space Core members for a task force to be led by me. Together we will find a Human, and the salvation of our system."

More cheering.

As usual, the Acamarians' plans were proceeding perfectly. Of course, getting the Bihamie, Wessen, and Kraz to cooperate with each other for more than five standard minutes on board a ship would try even the best Acamarian's skills. None of the species got along well, and the Bihamie especially were contentious by nature. It was a good thing Raan was the finest Arbitrator his species had recently seen.

Raan walked onto the bridge of the ship to find his crew already arguing. Qasalas's hackles stood on end— dark brown fur ruffled up from the rest of her tawny coat. Her tail lashed and she practically had her claws out, as if she was ready to leap into the safety of the jungle trees that covered her home planet. She, like many Wessen, was a talented fighter and Raan had put her in charge of security, as well as being their pilot.

Kaj's shoulder scales flushed dark purple, making them stand out from the green scales that made up the rest of his skin. The thick scales protected his people on their icy homeworld and displayed emotion. He also bared his claws and snarled. The Bihamie was his engineer. It seemed both of them were angry at Nashira, his Kraz science officer.

The Kraz blinked violet eyes that looked enormous from the distortion of the clear-plas helmets they wore. It contained the gases needed to keep them breathing, circulated with a pack they wore on their back. Nashira had their arms crossed, a sign of their agitation as they unconsciously protected the tubes that kept them alive outside of their gas giant world.

"Hello, crew," Raan said.

After a few more snarls and shouts they fell silent and turned to look at him. Kaj's shoulders faded to a more neutral brown and Nashira relaxed their guard. It took a moment longer, but Qasalas smoothed her hackles.

"You all know how important our mission is." He gestured in the general direction the Conquerors would come from. "We're not going to accomplish it if we don't work together. We must find a Human. To do this, we will have to learn to think as a Human does. I've uploaded files to each of your data centers. Study them. Learn them. Our first destination is Cignus Two, the last known location of a Human colony. It will take us some time to get there. We will use this time to learn about Humans. Any questions?"

The others stared at him, as if trying to accept that they would have to take orders from a pale skinned, big headed Acamarian. All three species used his as arbitrators, but none actually took commands from his people. Well, not that they realized, anyway.

Raan smiled. "Very well. We depart in thirty standard minutes. Dismissed."

Without further comment, each left the bridge to prepare for departure.

Raan sat down into the captain's chair. The Bihamie had provided the scout ship, so the chair was much wider than he required, and his longer legs meant his knees were bent awkwardly, but he wouldn't have given up this position for anything. Adding captain of the mission that would save his people to his list of titles was a tremendous opportunity. One he didn't intend to waste.

A loud *clang* echoed down the tube leading to the engine compartment, followed by fierce cursing. The Bihamie were brilliant engineers, but quick to anger.

Harrumphing, Raan stood to check the readouts. He simply hoped that the entire crew could cooperate long enough to find a new Human colony. It would have been much easier to use a single species crew, but his plan depended on the disharmony the mixed crew would create. He just had to hold them together for a short time. Throwing his narrow shoulders back, he headed toward engineering to start phase two of his plan; getting his crew to think: "What would Humans do?"

"Kaj, what's wrong?" Raan ducked slightly to enter the engineering compartment.

"This..." he snarled something in his own language that Raan knew was quite uncomplimentary. "It's broken. We won't make our departure window." He kicked the bulkhead. The high pitched screech from his claws on the metal made Raan wince.

"Remember what I said about thinking like a Human?"

"I have not the time for your silly document when our launch looms and my equipment is broken," Kaj growled.

"I will read the passage." Raan touched his wrist

band and the document appeared, projected before him. "Humans bond with their machines emotionally. When the machines stop working, Humans will pet the machine and feel sad for it."

"That is ridiculous. It is mere metal." Kaj's shoulder scales brightened to orange with scorn.

"Yet these Humans have done what no one else has and defeated the Conquerors."

Kaj's scales shifted to neutral brown while he thought before becoming a light blue of embarrassment. "I will try. Do not mock me."

"Never." Raan inclined his head and crossed his slender arms. "Perhaps if you pretend it is a Bihamie spawn?"

"Yes, of course." Kaj gurgled deep in his throat and patted the offending piece of machinery. Then he made a few scratchy cooing sounds and ran his claws lightly across the conduit.

Inwardly, Raan smirked, but he showed no sign of his amusement. That would defeat the plan.

After a moment of cooing, Kaj straightened, his shoulder scales brightening to light pink triumph. "I have found the problem. We shall depart on time."

"Well done, Kaj. We will find the Humans and defeat the Conquerors."

Kaj nodded, his scales fading to brown as he concentrated on fixing the ship.

Raan sat in the captain's chair and watched as the others prepared for departure. Qasalas and Nashira completed final systems checks. Kaj walked onto the bridge cooing gravelly nonsense words to a small box.

"What are you doing?" Qasalas demanded.

"Humans bond emotionally with their machines. When they aren't working they treat them like sick spawn, to assist in repair." Kaj's shoulder scales stayed a soothing green several shades lighter than the rest of his scales.

"That is preposterous," Nashira said.

"It works. We would not be leaving on time had I not expressed emotional sympathy to the particle conduit, allowing me to repair it efficiently." For a species so quick to anger, it was impressive how well Kaj kept his composure.

"Remember," Raan interjected. "We must constantly ask ourselves 'what would Humans do?' This is how we will accomplish our mission."

Kaj nodded and took his seat. He opened the small box and began repairing it with the tool kit he wore around his midsection.

Qasalas and Nashira traded bemused glances. Finally, Qasalas shrugged and took the controls. "We are ready to depart, Captain."

Raan tried not to show his pleasure at the title, keeping his features serene. "Clear to depart."

The thrust shoved them back in their seats until the compensators engaged and equalized the pressure. He saw Nashira check the readouts on their life suit. The Kraz homeworld had a volatile, high-pressure atmosphere and they needed to wear their suits while away from the gas giant. Though Raan hadn't heard of a suit failure in many years, the Kraz were wise to monitor them closely.

He watched through the viewport as the docking bay receded. The image switched to the rear at the touch of a button. The space station—considered neutral territory by all four races—spun gently to generate gravity. The giant ring and central spoke systems were one of the few places where their species frequently interacted. Arguments were common.

Raan switched the view forward and studied the screen. Currently there wasn't much to see, just black empty space, but before long the shipyard would come into sight. There they would pick up their jump ring for interstellar travel.

Intersystem travel was reasonably quick, but getting to their target system would take far too long without the jump ring technology. The ring fit around the midsection of the ship and bent space around the vessel, folding space and time and making the trip take weeks instead of lifetimes.

Raan would need those weeks to continue shaping his crew.

"They brought me along to protect the Human," Qasalas snarled. Her hackles bristled and she bared her claws.

Nashira folded their arms across their chest and backed away. "My suit is delicate. Were we to encounter enemies…"

"Qasalas, Nashira, what would Humans do?" Raan interrupted when he came across the altercation.

They both looked at him.

Harrumphing, he keyed up the document. "Humans go to great lengths to protect anyone they've pack-bonded with. This includes anyone they spend substantial time around."

"Treat crew as pack?" Qasalas frowned, tail lashing.

"Yes," Raan nodded.

Qasalas's tail twitched and her whiskers quivered for several more moments before she nodded. She stepped forward and brushed her arm against Nashira's before turning toward Raan.

"What are you doing?" Nashira stepped away.

Qasalas walked over to Raan and repeated the gesture, almost knocking him over and leaving hairs all over his jumpsuit.

"Treating you as pack, as a Human would do. We

Wessen rub against each other as part of our pack associations," Qasalas rumbled deep in her throat.

"Very well." Nashira shook their head.

"This means I will protect my pack to the best of my ability." Qasalas didn't even sound begrudging, as if she truly accepted the others as pack because a Human would.

Remarkable, Raan thought.

"Thank you," Nashira said after a slight hesitation.

Qasalas brushed against Nashira again before heading toward engineering. "I must find Kaj."

Raan moved to follow but Nashira intercepted him.

"I must show you something," they said.

Raan inclined his head slightly in acknowledgement and followed Nashira to their lab.

"I have been studying what little we know of Human customs. I am most confused by this one." They sat in a desk chair and used the holo to bring up an image of a small, twisted plant in a square pot.

"It is said that Humans find great pleasure in cutting the limbs from this, um, bonsai plant. I do not understand why they trim it in such a manner."

Raan thought fast. *Why would Humans want to trim a plant?* He mentally scanned the document before finding a plausible answer. "You must touch it to understand."

Nashira pulled their hands back to their chest and clenched them into fists. "Touch it?"

"Humans love to touch things. It is part of how they bond with their world."

Nashira's eyes widened. On their planet touching the wrong thing could mean death.

Kraz were not a tactile species.

"It won't hurt you. It's a holo." Raan tried to sound encouraging.

Pursing their lips, Nashira nodded and changed the settings on the holo, making it solid.

The bonsai image would react as the computer

thought it should when touched. Then Nashira pulled off one of their gloves, revealing translucent orange skin and squat fingers.

They hesitantly brushed their fingers across the top of the bonsai before their eyes widened again. "This is not unpleasant."

Raan inclined his head. "I will leave you to it."

Nashira nodded absently, studying the plant and running their hand through the small branches.

Raan had no idea if that was what a Human would do with a bonsai, but as long as it kept Nashira happy, that was what mattered.

Raan studied his crew. They stood assembled on the bridge for their final Human lesson. He had saved the hardest for last. Nashira carried the bonsai holo everywhere and had the others petting it, too. Kaj cooed to the engines constantly—admittedly they also ran smoother than normal—and Qasalas...Raan would never get all the tawny fur off of his jumpsuit. More amazingly, they were all getting along. That was almost unheard of.

"I've gathered you for the final lesson."

They regarded him, excitement evident in their postures, dilated eyes, and scale color.

"This is the most vital lesson of all: the hug. It is said that Humans hug frequently. It may even be necessary for their survival as a species. For certain, it is how they seal their pack bonds."

The others looked on eagerly. Raan prepared himself for the demonstration.

"Nashira, I'm going to put my arms around you. This is a hug."

Nashira took a step backward before glancing at the bonsai holo. They inhaled deeply before setting the holo down.

Raan stepped forward and put his arms around Nashira, careful not to bump his large cranium on their clear-plas helmet. He squeezed gently.

"Now you do the same." He kept his arms around Nashira.

After a brief hesitation, they finally returned the gesture.

"This is a very vulnerable position," Qasalas pointed out.

"Yes. It is a demonstration of the trust in a pack bond," Raan replied. He released Nashira and stepped back. They looked thoughtful.

"Now you all try," he ordered.

The others hesitantly embraced one another. Qasalas went so far as to rub her cheek against her crewmates while hugging them.

Raan did his best not to brush away the fur she left, lest he offend her and ruin the lesson.

Once everyone had practiced the hug with each other, Raan inclined his head in satisfaction. "You have all done well. Practice this, and everything else you have learned, and we will find the Humans! Once we have mastered hugging, there is also something called a group hug. We will practice when you are more comfortable with a simple hug."

The others shared glances before turning their attention back to Raan.

"We arrive at the Cignus Two tomorrow at 0800 standard."

"And the Humans will lead the way against the Conquerors!" Kaj said, shoulder scales turning pink in triumph. Qasalas purred happily and Nashira picked up their bonsai holo and passed it around for everyone to touch.

Raan settled into the captain's chair. His plan was coming together nicely.

The habitat domes on Cignus Two were similar to the ones his own people lived in. The Humans seemed to require the same amenities—beds, chairs, hydroponics—but all on a different scale than Raan's people. He shivered and wrung his hands, the strange almost-right proportions making him wish for home.

Qasalas, Nashira, and Kaj moved about, touching, cooing at, and rubbing against everything that had been left behind as they imagined Humans would. Raan doubted Humans took it to the extreme his crew did, but he wasn't about to discourage them.

Nashira called everyone into one of the domes. "It looks like they grew food here," they said. "The next room over looks important, too. It is heavily decorated."

They all went into the indicated dome and ran their hands and claws over the surfaces.

"They like this blue color," Kaj said looking at a painting on the wall.

"Though not the same color as our sky, it is a sky," Qasalas said. "See, these are strangely colored trees. What if their sun is a different color than ours? Perhaps they would look for a world with a similar sun."

"What kind of sun?" Kaj asked. "Can you tell?"

"From the spectrum of the lights in the domes and the clues from the painting..."

Nashira trailed off, punching data into their wrist band. "Yes. Yellow. Their sun is yellow."

"They like trees." Qasalas touched the painting again. "I've seen other pictures with trees and mountains. They must like worlds like mine."

"We require a yellow sun with a planet in the vegetation zone like yours," Nashira mumbled as they put in more data. "We have three possibilities within a reasonable distance of our location. However, we do not have time to search all three. We must think like them. Where would they choose to go?"

Raan let them work. His people hadn't considered the problem from this perspective, and he found himself agreeing with his crew's logic. The decision to include the others was wise.

"They probably had surveys, and Tian Three has reasonably docile animal life. Humans could pet them. They went to that world," Kaj finally said.

The others agreed at once.

"Are you certain?" Raan asked.

"Yes. Along with fuzzy animals to pet, this world has trees and water and many pleasing surfaces. Siran Two and Helos Four are not as advanced. While they contain living things, the life is slime molds and not petable," Nashira said.

Raan could think of many reasons why the last two worlds would have been preferable, but he kept that to himself. "When were those surveys completed?"

"Many years before humans occupied this colony," Nashira said after checking the data.

"If you are certain, we shall go there." Raan hoped his crew was correct, but it was a world his people had not searched.

"We are certain it is what the Humans would do," Qasalas said.

"I will go prepare the coordinates. Take one last look around and meet back at the ship in thirty standard minutes.

"I should like to pet a real plant," Raan overheard Nashira saying as he left.

Kaj gave a gravelly laugh. "The Humans will want to pet Qasalas. She is furry."

Qasalas rumbled, "Then I will pet them back."

Raan shook his head. He hoped his teachings hadn't gone too far.

"Hugs! This victory calls for hugs," Kaj was saying as Raan passed out of hearing distance. He harrumphed.

The crew had grown increasingly excited over the last few weeks of travel, coming up with questions to ask the Humans beyond how to defeat the Conquerors. They hoped the translators everyone used would cope with the Humans' language, or that the Humans had some exposure to one form or another of the trade language that many of the starfaring races had developed. Raan suspected they would have a way to communicate.

Another concern was disease transmission, but they had taken all the standard precautions developed over millennia of star travel, and that was rarely an issue so long as protocols were followed.

The four of them stood on the bridge as Qasalas disengaged the ring field and they dropped into normal space. Deceleration would take a day, but they could take readings immediately. Nashira consulted their computers and studied the readings. Kaj came over behind them while Qasalas continued to pilot.

"There are life readings consistent with the last survey." Nashira fell silent, studying the readouts.

"And?" Kaj finally asked.

Raan felt his circulation rate rise in anticipation.

"There are structures that have resemblance to the pictures we observed on Cignus Two. The computers detect life signals consistent with what we know of Humans," said Nashira.

They all cheered, even Raan.

"You have all done very well," Raan said. "We must prepare ourselves. It would be most helpful if we can convince one of them to return with us."

"Do you think one of them would?" Qasalas's fur rippled in excitement.

"I hope so, for all our sakes," Raan said.

Qasalas set the ship down gently. Already, bipedal creatures that resembled the few known images of Humans were coming out of the buildings and gathering near the ship. The structures looked simple, but signs of advanced tech showed here and there: electric lights, powered vehicles, and other modern conveniences similar to what Raan's own people might use. The settlement was built in a flat area near a water source and one of the many forests.

Raan had only been on a non-artificial world once and he hadn't enjoyed the experience. As the hatch opened, similar sensations assaulted him: moist air, smells, noise, air that moved on its own. He shuddered, but they needed a Human, so he hid his distaste.

Qasalas, Nashira, and Kaj had already descended the ramp so he joined them.

The group of humans who stared back at his crew wore simple plain clothing though their head fur—hair if he remembered correctly—and skin tones varied considerably. He thought he could pick out different genders and thought perhaps the very short were the Humans' young. It could be so hard to tell with aliens sometimes. The Kraz, for example, were much taller when they formed, pressed to their adult size by the atmosphere.

Realizing his crew waited for him, Raan stepped forward and held out his hands in a universal gesture for peace; fingers splayed, palms up to show empty hands.

After a moment a Human with darker skin and long, gray hair stepped forward. The human used a stick to assist in their walking and they hooked it over their arm and repeated the gesture. "Hello."

The translators worked!

"Hello," Raan replied. "We have come for your aid."

This caused a stir as several of the taller Humans stepped in front of the shorter ones.

"Help. We have come for your help." *What had the translator told them?*

"Oh," the Human who had greeted them said, "Of course. Welcome."

His crew exchanged glances. Kaj's shoulder scales went the brightest pink Raan had ever seen. He went forward, hands out. When the Human didn't back off he wrapped the Human in a hug.

Raan's eyes widened. The Humans stirred again but the one being hugged laughed after a moment and hugged Kaj back.

"It is nice to meet such friendly strangers," the Human said.

Nashira and Qasalas stepped forward as well and all gave hugs.

"Come, we must know what help it is you seek. We will go to the meeting hall."

Getting their help couldn't be that easy? Could it?

Bewildered, Raan followed the others. Small Humans ran up and touched Qasalas, laughing. She hugged them as well. This made the small ones laugh even more and rush about touching and hugging everyone. Raan endured the contact. *Perhaps Humans did touch as much as his crew seemed to think.* No matter, soon they would be back on their safe, and sterile, ship; hopefully with a Human along for the ride.

"I am Sita, an elder of our colony."

"Raan, captain of this mission, Kaj our engineer, Qasalas who is our pilot and our security, and Nashira who is our scientist," Raan introduced everyone.

"It is a pleasure to meet you all. What brings you to our world? You mentioned you need assistance?" Sita smiled.

Raan was starting to think Sita was one of the Human females. The one that sat next to her seemed to be male. A small furry creature that might have been a distant relative of Qasalas sat on his lap and rumbled.

The creature had excited his crew, especially as the Human did indeed pet it. Apparently, his sources were correct. Humans did touch everything.

"The Conquerors have returned. You are the only species who have defeated them. We want your secret, and your help to push them away from our worlds," Raan said.

The Humans shared glances before Sita spoke. "That was a long time ago and none here but myself remember those times. I was a young officer in the fleet. I will tell you all that I know."

"Perhaps you would come with us?" Raan almost held his breath.

She conferred quietly with the man holding the purring mammal before answering. "Yes, that would be acceptable. I presume you will return me once the conflict is over?"

Raan inclined his head. "Of course. We have much to learn from each other but we would not keep you longer than necessary."

She put her hands together in front of her. "I haven't been to space in many years. I look forward to it. Is tomorrow soon enough? Would you do us the honor of accepting our hospitality tonight?"

Raan inclined his head again. "It would be our honor."

Qasalas and Nashira whispered together before seeming to gain some resolve.

"Can we touch the creature?" Qasalas pointed to the small mammal.

Nashira spoke up, "And I should very much like to touch a bonsai. Do you have one?"

Sita's smile widened. "Yes, of course."

Sita settled in quickly, obviously used to shipboard life. Her walking stick didn't seem to slow her down and she happily answered any questions the others posed her. Raan was amazed at the change in his crew over the weeks together. No arguments, no disputes, only friendliness. The small bonsai plants Sita had brought the entire crew had gone a long way toward winning them over and convincing them that his teachings had been correct.

They were so excited to learn more from Sita, they overlooked some of the small details, such as how she didn't actually touch everything like his crew had begun to do. It seemed only the children had to experience the world that way.

From his observations during the evening he had spent with the humans, they also didn't seem to hug as much as the crew had taken to. He would never get Qasalas's hair off of his jumpsuit, but it was a small price to pay for freedom.

He leaned over the computer and input new coordinates. Soon this would all be over.

Raan sat in the captain's chair studying the distorted view of space through the ring field when the others came onto the bridge.

"We noticed that the coordinates were wrong," Qasalas said.

"We aren't going back to our system yet," Raan answered. It was early to reveal the final phase of his people's plan but they would need to know soon enough.

"Why?" Kaj asked, scales shifting to an agitated black.

"We made a deal with the Conquerors. They will leave our system alone in return for a Human. That's why we needed to find them."

The others traded glances before stepping in front of

Sita. Perhaps he had done his job too well.

"The Humans know how to defeat the Conquerors," Nashira said.

"Yes, but this way leads to a peaceful solution."

"For how long?" Qasalas growled. "They will want our worlds eventually. Better to fight them off so they don't ever return."

He had done his job too well. He thought quickly. "How many of your spawn will never see their first snow trek if war comes to our system?" Raan looked at Kaj.

The Bihamie's scales flashed to dark purple and he rumbled menacingly.

"We can stop this without a fight," Raan said. "Nashira, your people will fall first in a fight. Your suits are vulnerable in a way the Conquerors will exploit without mercy."

The Kraz stepped back and crossed their arms over their chest, shoulders hunched.

"And Qasalas, the Wessen world will be their prize. Strongly in the vegetation zone, they'll take it from your people and strip it of resources until they've used it up, as they do with any other planet they come across. We have to protect our system. Let others fight off the Conquerors. We can preserve our ways of life without the devastation of war."

Qasalas flexed her fingers, splaying claws. Growling softly, the Wesson looked ready to fight.

"We can't let the Conquerors have our worlds," Kaj snarled.

"You can't stop them," Raan said.

Nashira shivered. "We will stay hidden in our world. They can not take our resources, our planet is too inhospitable."

"They will enslave you through your weakness," Qasalas said, glaring at Nashira. "Then they will get your resources as well as ours."

Raan smiled. His words had broken their fragile new

ways and made them revert to their old, argumentative selves. He hadn't done his job too well after all. *Excellent.*

Sita stepped forward and carefully took Qasalas's and Kaj's clenched hands. "If my life will save all of yours..." The others stopped arguing over whose species would fall first and looked at Sita. "I will go." Sita's shoulders tensed and Raan guessed she wasn't happy about the idea.

He hadn't expected her to go willingly.

The others remained quiet for a moment longer, as if struggling with something.

Raan was about to speak and further the disruption when Nashira interrupted him.

"No!" Nashira said.

As if they'd rehearsed the maneuver, his crew all stepped closer and put their arms over each others shoulders.

Raan stared. *Were they actually...? They were!* He never thought he'd see the day such a disparate group of beings would get along—let alone group hug.

The four stared at him. "Even if we were willing to give up one of our pack..." Nashira said.

"Which we're not," Qasalas interjected.

"It's not what a Human would do," Kaj finished.

"Besides," Qasalas said, "the Conquerors will come back, and next time they'll want more, and more, until we are nothing but their slaves. Better to fight, and perhaps die, than live like that."

Raan's resolve wavered. Qasalas had a point. His peoples attempt to deal last time hadn't worked out so well, and if his crew could learn to work together...maybe...Kaj took Raan by one of his arms and Nashira by the other, pulling him into their circle.

"You taught us these things," Kaj said. "With Sita's help we can defeat the Conquerors and live free of fear."

Raan shook his head to clear his thoughts. "Sita, how did the Humans defeat the Conquerors?" Somehow they hadn't gotten around to asking that vital question yet.

Sita smiled. "There was some strategy involved that I will share, but essentially, we pulled all of humanity's different factions and ships into one fleet, assigned a talented commander and..." She hesitated. "We all worked together. We had a large enough fleet that together we could stand against them. Their strategy is to divide and conquer. It doesn't work when everyone cooperates and fights back together."

Raan stared. That was the big secret? Ridiculous. But...all the changes he'd seen on the ship, simply because they had tried to emulate Humanity. Maybe they *could* stand together long enough to defeat their enemy.

"Raan, we can do it. Together, we will do what the Humans did, and with Sita's guidance we can defeat the Conquerors," Qasalas said.

Strangely, Raan started to feel a shard of hope. It went against all reason, but if his crew could learn to work together peacefully, perhaps the rest of their peoples could as well.

He put his arms over Nashira and Kaj's shoulders, returning the hug. He let the feelings of togetherness bolster his growing hope. "Yes. We can. I will alter our course. By doing what the Humans did we will gain our freedom—together."

THEN THERE WAS GINNY

Sydney Seay

When my people made first contact with the Earthens, they anticipated there'd be panic. They anticipated the possibility of war, and outrage, and crisis—it's quite the unsettling thing, learning you are not alone in the universe. It's dangerous, introducing yourself to an isolated species, but necessary. If you don't introduce yourself, the backlash of them finding you on their own can be catastrophic.

My father was on the mission to acclimate the Earthens to intergalactic existence; he was among the party responsible for technological assessment. With all the satellites and baubles they'd been sending into their space, the decision to acclimate Earthens was more precautionary than out of a strict desire to meet them. If left alone any longer, they might have found us themselves. He used to tell me stories, about those early days, when they started to realize the Earthens were not like anything they'd known before.

"They're so curious," he told me once. "They're so curious, some of them dedicate their *lives* trying to learn what happened to people dead for centuries."

They thought it silly—all the members of integrated space. They thought it silly, all the way up to the moment the first archeology teams touched down on their home planets. Sifting and sorting the dirt and rubble of the past into narratives so real, you could almost hear the voices of the ages gone whispering in your ear.

In those early years, they called the Earthens the Child Species, because of the unrelenting, incessant curiosity they carried with pride. And they treated them like children; humoring silly whims, and dumbing things down to unnecessarily simple levels.

And when no one was looking, the Earthens seeped into every crack of the accessible universe.

"You know, they don't call themselves Earthens," my dad told me once, over dinner. "They call themselves *humans*. Isn't that an odd thing? For a species with such an uncanny ability to live anywhere, pleasant or not, they get attached to their homes. Rebuild them, even if nature knocks it down over and over...and yet they don't even link themselves to their planet."

I'd heard a lot about Earthens growing up on Zarsis. Father was always going away to work with them, bringing back stories and trinkets. Most of the trinkets were silly little things that the Earthens had given father as parting gifts, or as presents to pass on. Bracelets and charms, and culturally significant items that meant nothing to me but a lot to them. But if I was really lucky, I'd get a picture. Photographs were the epitome of human sentiment—a memory wasn't enough, they needed a snapshot of time and space on a glossy card to truly, happily remember the past.

Despite all I knew and had, it wasn't until I left Zarsis with a small exploration team that I truly got to know the Child Species.

There was an archeologist on board the ship, with pink skin and yellow hair and green eyes. She was all color and exuberance. A nasty scar tore a line up her neck, and a past adventure had cost her two fingers on her left hand, but she still smiled and joked, like it wasn't painful or permanent or ugly.

"Now I'm always spreading love," she said once, like missing her middle and ring finger had anything to do with emotion. But it made her laugh, and that laugh was music, and color, and vibrance.

That surprised me most about the humans; the color. So many different colors on their body, and not all humans had the same skin or hair or eyes, each one was a unique mix of textures and colors. They were born with so many colors, and then they added more with patterned clothes or jewelry. The Archeologist, Ginny Adams, had three holes in each earlobe. Holes she *put there*, to fit even more baubles on her body.

I went down onto a planet with Ginny once, for something called an excavation. She tried to explain it to me, but as far as I could tell, it was grave robbing people who had been dead a very long time.

Kenzic 17 was one of many previously inhabited planets in the Orsus Galaxy. The civilizations had died out long ago, and no other intelligent life was developed enough in that system to warrant going back there. That is until the humans came, with endless questions and curiosity.

"You see, burial rituals can tell you a lot about a culture." Ginny said, taking pictures of an old, dusty tomb.

"Back on Earth, so much of the Ancient Egyptians is known primarily through their burial rights. What they thought was important, how they perceived the relationship between life and death. One of the oldest, grandest landmarks on Earth are the Pyramids of Giza, and when it comes right down to it, they're just huge tombs for the Pharaohs." She brushed dust off a large, ornate casket while she spoke, the small bristle brush sending clouds of dust into the air around her. "They filled the tomb with everything the Pharaoh would need in the afterlife.

They separated the organs into canopic jars designed to look like protective deities. The bodies were mummified, because the Egyptians believed that in the afterlife the soul was reunited with the body, before Osiris. The only organ left in the body during mummification was the heart."

"Why?" I asked, handing her the decontamination containers.

She smiled at me while she put the dressings and items from the tomb into their protective containers. I don't know if it was a human thing or a Ginny thing, but she always seemed to leave something unstated when she got talking; a little piece to the story she didn't disclose, just to see if you'd ask. A little test, to see if you'd leave it be, or seek out the extra knowledge.

"To be weighed, and judged, in the afterlife."

It always made her happy when I sought out the unstated piece. It made her smile, a gentle lift of her lips without teeth which served no real purpose but to brighten the eyes. I liked when she smiled, but I liked when she didn't more. When she was focusing on the tomb, or the rubble that meant something only to her, you could see her mind working. She scrunched her face up, rather than stretching it, and that was when I found Ginny the most pleasant.

After the excavation of Kenzic 17, you would be hard pressed to find Ginny anywhere outside her lab. She was always sketching and scribbling in notebooks, mumbling to herself about the objects and what they could mean. Humans liked to talk—even if only to themselves. She cleaned centuries of dirt off coins and jewelry with a touch I'd almost dare call loving, for the simple driving reason of curiosity. It would get so bad at times that someone would have to go in and drag her out for a meal. The Chef went into the lab once, with a plate of food, and he spent the next week cleaning it out of crevices no one knew he even had. No one repeated that endeavor—no one had the guts.

"You see, son," dad had told me once when I was sick and bored, "humans get very possessive about things that don't make sense. Once a human gets attached to something, no matter what it is, they'll protect it with the ferocity most species preserve for protecting their young."

"That's weird," I had replied, unable to wrap my head around the concept—especially when my mind was fuzzy with sickness.

"It's odd, I'll admit. But if a human gets attached to *you*? There is no companion who will do more or care more for you, than a human who considers you their friend. Even a human who considers you an acquaintance is a powerful ally."

I always thought he was exaggerating. I should have known better, my father didn't exaggerate anything. How happy he was, and not how mad he was—you could always know exactly where you stood with my father, so why would he say anything but the truth about the humans? It took Ginny Adams protecting her excavated artifacts like a wild animal protects their young, to prove that point to me.

The most interesting thing about Ginny's companionship wasn't how attached she got to me, or the artifacts. It wasn't her propensity to stretch her face with smiles, or scrunch it up in concentration, or always— *always*—wanting to talk about something, or share a thought or knowledge. Rather, it was how I found myself enjoying that companionship.

Immensely.

Ginny brought me to a human colony during a two day leave at Ruzu. It was a temperate planet, with good light and nice swimming holes, where a lot of expeditions went for full crew leaves. A couple of human stores and services had quickly cropped up all over the galaxy once they were introduced to integrated space. This particular crop-up became a small colony that Ginny called Chinatown.

"This happens all the time." she smiles, leading me by the hand through the crowds of people.

"Chinatown, Little Italy, Koreatown. Similar culture, similar beliefs, a common language; we seek out people who are like us when we're in unfamiliar places. Makes us more comfortable."

"Then why go anywhere?" I asked, distracted by a snippet of language I didn't understand.

"Why not? People build little communities like this for comfort, but they're still leaving for a reason. Financial stability. Curiosity. A better future for their children—America has places like this all over, but that doesn't invalidate the purpose of moving."

She stopped us in front of a store with pictures in the windows, and the glowing word *TATTOO*. She squeezed my hand, though I didn't know why, and pushed through the door. A tiny little bell sounded. I didn't know what a tattoo was, but there was an annoying buzzing filling the room, and pictures all over the walls.

Ginny Adams was expected.

She sat in a black chair coated in plastic after a brief conversation and a few signatures. I followed close behind her, feeling very much out of place and very confused. I couldn't tell if Ginny didn't tell me what she was doing because she assumed I'd know, or because she assumed I'd ask.

Ginny always did love questions.

"What is this place?" I finally asked after a man with medical gloves started to swab at her wrist.

"A tattoo parlor," she said, like I had any clue what that was.

Something in my face must have given away my

confusion, because her mouth stretched and her eyes compressed into a delightfully odd expression that I couldn't put an emotion to. They have a wider range than any other species I'd ever met—some didn't even have words in my native tongue. It was like looking right at a new color, observing its existence without being able to quantify it, or even describe it to yourself. It just was, and it was strange and uncomfortable, and kind of beautiful, too.

"When you get a tattoo, a really fast moving needle injects ink under the skin. It's something humans of all cultures have been doing for centuries, it's just gotten a little different as technology evolved."

That night I watched a man hurt Ginny over and over with a fast, tiny stabbing machine. I watched her scrunch her face up in pain—*voluntary pain*—while a small design appeared, the black ink burrowing into her skin. They would bead up, ink and blood, painting a vibrant, macabre abstract on her pale wrist. The beads were quickly wiped away, their brief existence giving life to the permanent fixture of ink under Ginny's skin. It was a horrifying, magnificent spectacle.

"That's *permanent*?" I asked, over a bowl of something called lo mein.

"Pretty permanent," she snorted, using the sticks to eat like they were actually utensils and not starvation tools.

"What is it?"

The noodles I managed to balance slipped off the end of the stick, back into the bowl. Ginny snorted, and shoved a different utensil at me: one with prongs that was much more familiar. The food wasn't bad, once I could actually get it to my mouth. Different, but not bad.

"It's the Eye of Horus. An Ancient Egyptian symbol of health, and protection," she said, pulling a small, curly pink thing out of the bowl. She popped it in her mouth, like she was giving herself a little time to think about whether she wanted to say anything more. Finally, she swallowed the mystery item I'd been picking around, and decided to divulge more. "My grammy did a lot of work with the Ancient Egyptians, in her day. She taught me all about them, even took me to see the pyramids. Grammy's why I became an archeologist. The stories of Egypt, the tales of their lives and culture...it's a huge part of my life. Makes me feel closer to her....You know? Besides"—she smiled again, this time teeth and all— "it's a big, cold universe out there. Couldn't hurt to have a little extra protection along the way."

Ginny, like most humans, was a walking paradox. Intuitive, realistic, and logical, but bursting with emotion and carrying the ever-present weight of unwarranted superstition. But superstition doesn't always keep you safe. Humans had mixed feeling of the concept of fate and destiny, which to my people it is a fact. You cannot predict your fate, but it waits for you nonetheless.

It was destiny for the humans to integrate, and destiny for me to meet Ginny.

Ginny Adams, who taught me much about humans and color and easy joy. Ginny Adams, who smiled easily, and sought the answers to everything in dust and tombs. Ginny Adams, who saw the pyramids and stars, and excavated Kenzic 17. Ginny Adams, who put her faith in a symbol of the ancients, and it failed.

Emotions don't come easily to me, or my people—not the happy ones, not the good ones. But Ginny showed me her soul, and though I didn't show her mine, I felt it. I missed her companionship when she disappeared for weeks into the lab; I missed her stretched mouth and scrunched face. Humans grow attached easily to people and things, and there were billions of people in the universe like Ginny Adams, but none of them *were* Ginny

Adams. Humans grow attached, and so did I.

But destiny is brutal and fickle, and it doesn't care how you feel.

A close call with a meteor storm cracked our hull, barely a day's travel from our final destination. The old ship couldn't sustain the damage, and the crack sprouted fingers and offshoots. The ship was so old only one emergency escape module worked. It would fly, but there was a major problem with it.

Ginny Adams was a smart girl, and she figured out the problem before anyone else. She remembered, in the heat of the moment, the warning they'd gotten when they started the mission. She hung back and, before anyone knew what had happened, sealed the module from the outside. The module's automatic door operations were broken, and the only way to open or close the pod was from the outside. There wasn't time to fight about who would survive and who would die, no time to hesitate or no one survived—and she knew that.

So she sealed us in, and it didn't take long for the pilot to realize he couldn't open the door. Everyone was fighting. It was a cacophony, everyone yelling at her to open the door, for the pilot to open the door.

"I can't!"

For there to be a way, some way, *any way.*

"There has to be a way!"

"Just open the door!"

"There has to be—"

"Open the damn door!"

But there was no way.

The ship's hull gave way, forcing the pilot to release the module into space before depressurization sucked us further in. Destiny brought me to Ginny Adams, and destiny took her back.

Ginny went to the stars to explore the mysteries of life. She lived for questions and curiosity; a member of the Child Species, taking to the stars with remarkable ease. Ginny Adams was warm, and bright.

And Ginny Adams died, held in the cold palm of the universe.

Sometimes, something happens in your lifetime so big you couldn't imagine any other possibility. No one expected the humans, and no one wanted the humans. But once they were there? Once they stepped off that planet and into the stars, it was like you finally noticed something that had always been there.

My father grew up without humans, but the only childhood I can imagine without stories and baubles from them is a cold and lonely one. Ginny wasn't all humans, and not all humans were Ginny. Some are bitter and cold and full of just as much hate as Ginny was full of light and happiness. Not all members of a species are one and the same, especially with the unusually diverse cultures that came from that one little planet.

But I didn't meet those other humans. I met Ginny. And if anyone else had been there when the hull cracked and the module didn't function properly, they would have hesitated. We all would have died. I would have spent my life with Ginny Adams without a second thought, but instead she gave me her years.

It's always bothered me, that the woman who filtered the world through burial rituals and death rites wouldn't get a burial appropriate to her culture. But the universe claimed Ginny as its own. Maybe she was *too* good and happy and exuberant. The universe took care of Ginny's burial, and she'd spend her eternity excavating the stars. Or she'd learn the secrets of the universe from the bosom of a black hole. That's what I chose to believe—Ginny on one last adventure.

No matter how many people I meet, no matter what happiness I find in life, I always have and always will carry one regret. Despite all the baubles and trinkets I have lining the shelves of my home from humans my father met and knew, I never got one from Ginny. The vacuum of space took claim of her possessions as it took claim to her body and life.

I wish I had a picture of Ginny. She came into my life with such an unexpected force. A photograph would be tangible proof she actually existed; that she wasn't just a figment of my imagination. Maybe that's why humans are so fond of them—proof they have lived and loved. But there was no photograph of Ginny; with her two missing fingers and scar on her neck, the black ink on her wrist no longer a symbol I could recall, except that it was thick and bold, and when the needles passed over the tendons, she squeezed my hand tight in hers. There was no picture, no trinket.

There was only Chinatown and the tattoo parlor. The excavations and explorations of planets I never imagined I'd step foot on. I was left with borrowed memories of Egypt and Earth, and a face that would scrunch and stretch. She was there and then gone, filling a space in my life I never knew was empty until she filled it and then left.

Ginny Adams showed me the universe through a lens of curiosity and exploration. And all I had left when she was gone, was a memory of her smile, and the desire to hear her laugh one more time.

Because that laugh was music, and color, and vibrance.

THE DOWAGER

Richard A. Becker

"What nice caves you've made for yourselves," the Dowager said, looking at the apartment blocks whirring past. "Together and apart. Very contradictory. Very primitive." The elderly alien waited to see if her human servant would make any response, and though it was subtle, it was still satisfying.

Emma sighed.

Their transport passed through the human part of Portland and back across the river to the Lordly Nests of The Dowager's people. The simple-minded machine barreled along on reliable old wheels, threading its way through traffic as Emma listened to the running commentary from her employer. She wasn't paid nearly enough for the task of caring for her scaly charge, but it was a living wage, and at least her generation were employees, not chattel.

Despite knowing Polly would growl at her and The Dowager would be irritable for days if she noticed, Emma sometimes would secretly pet the warm, furry live creature—a chamerot, imported from her home planet—that coiled on The Dowager's upper body to give her warmth. She avoided the painful little flicks of the creature's curious barbed tongue, but she knew it loved to be petted, and she enjoyed petting it.

As they had for a decade and a half, Emma and The Dowager sat in the transport as it rumbled into the heavy duty lift and they were all lifted to the imperial heights of

The Dowager's home.

Emma had always somewhat admired The Dowager's airy nest-residence, though its architecture and furniture were strange to human proportions and physiology. It reminded her of a combination of a high cat perch and a connected bunch of bird nests, though it had other qualities which made it much more unearthly than that. Or perhaps it was earthly to her, after all, since she had seen Lordly Nests on media and in person all her life, just as every human in living memory had.

They walked in, past the security scans and the protection machines, and automated voices blessed and welcomed the mistress of the house, ignoring her servant entirely, of course. At one time, when her human's name had been Kuma, The Dowager had swept into her residence each evening with regal weight and speed. Now her walk had slowed to a waddle, and her servant was obliged to slow her long-legged stride to a respectful dawdle.

Emma lifted the sleepy chamerot from The Dowager's shoulders and back. The animal was getting old, though it was nowhere near as long-lived as its mistress. Its broad, flexible, rubbery body was deliciously warm, and its thick, soft fur was extraordinarily comfortable. The two mated pairs of dastedgynes that the old alien kept wrapped around her lower legs were less luxurious but equally warm. All of the animals were heavy, soft and docile as Emma transferred them into their cages, then watered and fed them.

The Dowager rattled her way into the main room while Emma cared for the kitchen menagerie. Her own cat, Polly, ate her wet food like lightning, as always. Just to put The Dowager off for a few more minutes, Emma took the time to put a packet of Katpops treats in the convection oven. Within half a minute, the little red pellets of condensed meat had popped into kitty treats, and Emma placed the open packet before Polly. The cat devoured them in record time. Emma carried Polly with her, to and from The Dowager's nest every day. It was good to have some terrestrial company, and Polly enjoyed hissing and spitting at the chamerots, which pretended Polly did not exist.

The alien ate simply, due to her easily unsettled digestion. Emma ceremoniously set down the cup before her dais and The Dowager took it up. The Dowager sipped as much of the egg whites as she could; they were fresh and cold in her homeworld-styled cup. She had always enjoyed them with certain special meals; Emma had watched her do this for years. It was still a little grotesque to her, but she'd made a connection years earlier, which had taken most of the queasiness away.

She tried, as she had every day now for almost a third of her life, to make idle conversation with The Dowager. Even now it was always a dicey proposition. There was never any certainty about which subjects the creature would consider harmless and which she would consider aggravating. Emma had long since given up on avoiding political matters, because The Dowager could, and did, make any discussion political. Because the alien's politics were always focused on alien over human, offworld over colonial, it was also always a losing proposition for Emma.

The Dowager had been spawned on Earth, as had nearly every member of her species still on the planet. Visits from her people had dwindled to a scattered rain of starships, as their collective interests had shifted in other directions. Humanity, like grass cut sharply against the soil, grew in all the empty places they had left behind. The Dowager felt about this as keenly as if she had ever lived in the glory days herself. She seemed to feel everything very keenly, as Emma saw it.

Emma was in the midst of making a passing comment on the weather, which was warming up and would doubtless make her employer happy, when The Dowager finished her eggs.

"Finished, human girl," she said. "Clean and go. I do not need you any more tonight."

It was early, and Emma couldn't really conceal her surprise. "Are you certain, Dowager? It's only 8:30."

"I am the daughter of many queens. I know what time it is. Clean and leave me."

"Yes, Dowager."

Emma did as the creature commanded, and when she left she felt, somehow, that The Dowager was trying to conceal one of her many strong feelings. It was unlike the alien, but then there was public transportation to wrestle with, her own dinner to eat, and maybe an Experience to take in before bed.

Every day, Emma walked past the local Scar. The aliens had made humanity leave the marks of their conquest intact in key places on the planet, as a kind of ongoing psychological warfare. But the same vast, gutted, glassy trenches that had ignited repeated revolts in her great-grandparents' days, daily bouts of white-hot fury in her grandparents' time, and heated rhetoric in her parents' youth, were now being quietly eliminated one by one—in Emma's adulthood. They didn't mean anything but an ugly, stupid waste to her. She pitied a culture so ignorant that they would ruin good land just to spite those born on it.

The whole Earth had once belonged to humanity, of course, or at least that had been how humans had seen it. Since the coming of The Dowager's species, people had divided themselves into two broad camps: Those who felt that ownership more fervently than ever, and those who accepted that a place was only a place, and everyone stood on a place far more than they really owned it.

Then again, the urge to divide into opposing factions

had been humanity's downfall for many generations, until the aliens had seized upon it in their invasion. Only the invaders had truly united the tool-using sapient life of Earth, though it had been much too late to prevent conquest. Perhaps a united Earth would have failed against superior technology anyway. Humans would never know, though that would not prevent eternal debate on the topic. And there was the urge to divide and dispute once again.

Much of the aliens' technology could not be reverse-engineered by humans because it was based on substances, and even spatial conditions, that did not exist anywhere on or near Earth. Without the interstellar culture to build the tools to build the factories, humans could only steal invader technology and use it until it failed. It smacked, to both humans and aliens, of cargo cults, hand-me-down culture and barbarity. Yet no barbarity was completely out of the question for either species, and so there had been failed rebellions again and again. Some called the dead combatants heroes, but they were still all dead, anyway.

Emma had nothing to do with any of that, and despite The Dowager's occasional implication about herself, she was confident that the old alien had never so much as seen a human/invader skirmish in person. On the rare occasion that an invader soldat had been seen in the streets of Portland, Emma had noted the telltale signs of excited fear in her employer. She could not tell if the creature was more reassured than alarmed by the military of her own species, but if she had been asked to wager, Emma would have put her money on fear.

Sometimes she suspected fear was always first in The Dowager's feelings. That, and an inhuman kind of loneliness that was completely at odds with The Dowager's natural territorial inclinations. Sometimes she tried to draw her employer out, very carefully offering ideas.

"There are still plenty of your people on Earth," said

Emma. "We could visit them."

"None of my friends are still alive," snapped The Dowager. "There is no one to visit."

"There are plenty of younger people of both of our species," said Emma. "You could make new friends."

"The younger people are idiots," raged The Dowager. "Yes, even of my kind! They act so much like your species, they're like beasts themselves! There is no one left who still knows the old ways. No one left who remembers how wonderful sspreeecchtt/cl was, or what to say when you m/hiii*, or even the gesture of the equinox. We've degenerated, and surely it is time for the final plague to claim us all. I see all the signs. It is time."

"How long have your people predicted the final plague would punish their degeneracy?" Emma smiled.

"Long enough. It is almost here," said The Dowager. "You probably look forward to it, twisted creature."

"No," said Emma. "I wouldn't wish that on anyone."

Emma was young by human standards. She was only in her forties now; in a human lifespan, that was barely past the end of the first third of her existence. Still, she had chosen to have a child when she was still in her prime years, not opting for the waiting list for a rejuvenated womb. Even though the aliens' Minimal Human Breeding program was well out of date, Earth had retained the cultural imperative to population control. And so one baby had been enough for Emma and her husband.

They had been fresh from college, cautiously optimistic about a world emerging from a great shadow. The two humans hadn't had much money, so their studies were practical and job-oriented: The male had become an accountant, and his mate, Emma, had become a xenocare specialist. They had loved and quarreled in the usual primate ways, finding community in one another, their families, and their little child. Death separated Emma from her man, and time took her baby away, as her offspring grew up to become a technician in one of the sprawling orbital cities that were increasingly occupied by nothing but humans. "Dirty skins pushing out clean scales," as The Dowager had put it. "Breeding like insects and destroying everything worthwhile."

Emma had a telecall from her child every Saturday, and there were family gatherings a few times a year. These were the times she loved best; even when they hadn't seen one another in what felt like a lifetime, every small gesture and nuance spoke of connection, sharing, and warmth.

Something had upset The Dowager's digestion. She had vomited up her meal, which had been a passel of furry live grub creatures from the kitchen menagerie. The macerated corpses were splayed out in a glossy blob of viscous digestive fluid. Throwing up was miserable for a human, but excruciating for the invaders, whose metabolisms were always difficult. If it had been possible, Emma would have sworn that The Dowager appeared to be embarrassed and a little frightened.

"Clean it up, lazy human girl," said The Dowager. Emma earned her keep and then some, as she did the tedious chore without a word. "If only humans hadn't been so lazy, you might have been worth something."

When Emma was done, she looked carefully at her employer. The creature was old, and clearly not in the best condition for her age, but was it worse than that?

"Impertinent servant, stop staring at me," The Dowager said, looking away. "Do your chores in the other chambers. Leave me."

"Yes, Dowager."

When The Dowager's skin had been sleek and she had been full of youth, long before Emma had existed, her conquering breed had fairly thronged the streets. All the signs and visuports were still in the alien language, and the human tongues of Hindi, French, and English had yet to resurge. She thought back sometimes, to those beautiful times, and lifting her voice in the evening chorus under the weird blue skies of Earth.

Now the evening chorus was only a ragged voice here and there, churring from a rooftop or a street corner. The younger conquerors resorted to infoplex connections, virtually chorusing together, but The Dowager found that too depressing to contemplate.

The simple transparent globe that was the traditional invader religious symbol, their sign of the Divine, was missing from its place in The Dowager's nest. Emma had not commented on its absence, but she knew she never moved it except to put it in the duster and then put it back. The spiritual sign was simply gone now, and Emma had known better than to ask about it.

"Your food is disgusting," said The Dowager, marveling at Emma's sandwich as if she had never seen one before. "Did your ancestors take up layers of detritus from a swamp and eat that?"

"No," said Emma. "We just find it more convenient to sometimes eat food between two pieces of bread."

"Yes, your bread," said The Dowager. "Ground plant matter made bulbous with fungus gas, then burned in a kiln."

"You make it sound so delicious," Emma said, taking another bite.

"Disgusting."

Emma had eaten her meals out of The Dowager's sight for years. The alien had recently given her new instructions: She needed Emma close by, and she would accustom herself to watching Emma's revoltingly articulate mouth chew and swallow her awful fodder. She passed the time while Emma's mouth was full by sneering at the disgraceful decline of the invader government and the way humans were taking over all the administrative posts as if it all belonged to them.

"It does belong to us," Emma had said between bites one day. "We evolved here."

"Typical," rasped The Dowager. "So stupid. If spawning someplace made it your home, no one would ever have left the Primal Spawning Place. Your place in the universe is wherever you take action. Not where your life begins and ends. Those are not actions you take. Those are things that happen to you. Slave thinking. Slave race."

"Slavery is over."

In Emma's grandmother's day, Earth had been a colony of The Dowager's people. In her mother's day, the Earth been changed to a protectorate status. Now, in the years since Emma had graduated from Portland Human College, the aliens had revised their own status to "supervisors in residence" and there was a provisional government that was autonomous in everything but name.

The Dowager muttered, "Gyooorr//hchhh *k!k* gyuuuuhuhuhuh," under her breath.

"You know I speak your language, Dowager," Emma said, quietly. "I humbly request that you please don't call me that name."

The Dowager feigned surprise for the ten-thousandth time. "'Speak my language,' it says. If it does speak the proud language of the victorious ones, it speaks it poorly. With a terrible accent."

"I'm sure I do," said Emma. "All the same, I repeat my request."

The Dowager made the sign of noncommittal avoidance, but she did not repeat the insult.

"We know that nothing is given," said The Dowager. "Everything is taken. Some of the time, you humans know this, too. But you are always infected with the gifting stupidity."

Emma took a moment to compose her thoughts. "Giving is also a strength, Dowager," she said. "I'm sorry to dispute you, but that is something *we* know to be true."

The Dowager made a sign of disgust. "You lost to us, you will always lose to us. When you die, you always beg your invisible ones for mercy. You expect something from everything, you think gifts will be given. We do not."

Emma was puzzled by the direction the conversation had taken. The Dowager was agitated, but her human servant couldn't see why.

"It's probably just one of our many flaws," Emma said. "We have to live and die with them."

"We are conquerors and rulers," said The Dowager. "I am the daughter of many queens. Many queens." She seemed to search for words, then: "For as long as we have had language, my people have always chosen to die in the proper way."

Emma had never discussed the topic with the alien before. "Yes, Dowager."

"It is the right way. You humans cluster together, with your stink and your gabble. We do not. We walk with the Divine. If there was always another with us, it would crowd out the light of Divinity. You understand?"

"I had heard something about that, Dowager."

"It is right that civilized creatures live and die in the company of the Divine, not crawling over one another like maggots."

"I don't dispute it."

"Good." She preened for a moment. "I have much to take pride in."

"Yes, Dowager."

The Dowager, like all her species, had mated upon achieving maturity. She had known the excitement of going to the same pandith that her mother had once visited, and working with the pandith to find just the right male to fertilize her eggs. Their courtship fortnight was a decadent, erotic heaven; each sunrise, the mating song; each sunset, the dance of pleasure.

On the thirteenth night, they had struggled in the hot mud; on the fourteenth morning, she had left her eggs and crawled away, limp and exhausted, knowing that he would soon spread them over with the stuff of life. Then, as modern custom dictated, her attendants had collected the fertilized eggs and preserved them to hatch later, one per year, for a decade.

Naturally, all of The Dowager's children had gone immediately to the very best stithaprashna, drawing upon their life-inheritances, and like their father, The Dowager never saw any of them again. It was the natural way of things.

It was true there had been a thousand indignities every day, all her life, thanks to the alien invaders, Emma could never deny that. Yet something inside her said there was more at stake in how she and all of humanity lived their lives now. Long ago, a Chinese writer had posted: *Now, first contact is every day. Now, we all speak for the whole human race, every day.*

Emma believed it. If history told her what humans had been, then she felt it was up to her—her life—to speak for what humans could still be.

Yet for all that, she still let the carping old creature draw her out sometimes.

She was on her hands and knees, scrazzing little bits of bacterial grit out from between the flooring tiles, while The Dowager declaimed at her in a cracking voice:

"If we had not claimed your planet," said The Dowager, "you would have languished for many more generations in ignorance, savagery, and greed. We've civilized you."

Emma was not in the mood. She looked up from her cleaning. "In some ways, yes," she said in measured tones. "But we had some civilization of our own as well. I'll never really know what it was like to live in world with nothing but humans. And you'll never know what it's like to live in a world without us."

"It's a dirty world," grimaced The Dowager. "Full of human simians who would breed themselves to death without our wisdom."

Emma almost replied: *You've never seen any other planet in person, any more than I have*, but she collected her thoughts. Then chose something much worse, as humans will often do.

Emma sat back on her heels, pausing in her work. "You like listening to our koto music and eating chicken" —*Raw*—"You go out to our hottest deserts and sun yourselves for weeks on end. You enjoy the smell of wood bark and the color of our rushing sunrise. You make the signs of cathartic sorrow at the sight of humans cuddling in their sleep."

The last comment drew The Dowager up in her seat, expressing indignation and growing anger. "I do not!"

"All your kind do," said Emma. "Because you all sleep the same way you eat...alone." She met The Dowager's gaze, as humans had feared to do, forty years earlier.

"And you don't like it."

The alien's claws swept across a nearby shelf, scattering and smashing tiny memory-pieces of the homeworld she had never seen, inscribed in a desperately complex language that she—like all her kind on their colonies, including Earth—had never spoken with the correct accents or ever completely learned to read.

"All your kind are violent, stupid children!" roared

The Dowager. "You sleep in your own disgusting skin
fluids and you stink of your heated food. You needed us!
We saved you from ignominy and death!"

The old alien's claws trembled with emotion and
exhaustion. She seemed to convulse in on herself, and
her trilobed eyes flicked this way and that, seeking her
ankusha. Her ankusha—which had been outlawed five
years before Emma had even been born—the traditional
means by which her species had kept rebellious humans
in their place. The Dowager had never used the cruel
device; she had only ever seen her parent use it a handful
of times, and she had learned to wave it, threaten with it,
but had strangely never acquired the taste for it.

In the midst of her harangue, The Dowager's voice
suddenly cut away to a faint gasp, as if she had been
grafted to a malfunctioning amplifier. Her body language
betrayed alarm, and her flesh emitted the scent of her
pain. The Dowager fell, helpless to the floor.

The physician, who had already left, had been a
human. The Dowager despised her, and cursed her
weakly and endlessly, but her original medical aide—a
creature like herself—had died years ago. The Dowager's
species did not like to take jobs in medicine, dentistry, or
anything else that required them to be subservient to the
bodily needs of another. Humans had no such bias, and
had quietly stepped into all such posts as they emptied
of their alien practitioners. It was one of the hundred
thousand complaints that The Dowager had about
modern life.

Emma pondered the bottle in her hand.

As the human doctor had departed, she had taken
Emma aside and spoken with her in pidgin French-Hindi,
as human servants had for generations.

"The old madame is terminally ill," she said. "Her

own people never found a cure for it. God damn us if we look for it on their behalf."

Emma nodded, but she didn't feel the same bitterness the physician did. The tide of conquest had been receding since her infancy; The Dowager symbolized something different to Emma than she did to the physician. Still, Emma had no desire to argue.

"Is there medicine for her? To make it easier?"

"We should euthanize the creature," the physician said, "but since that's against global regulations, give her this." She handed Emma a bottle full of a transparent fluid. "The directions are on the side. If it were a human being we were talking about, I'd say 'I'm sorry,' but as it is, I'll say good riddance to bad garbage." The doctor nodded her farewell to Emma and began to depart.

At the door, she said, "Regulations wouldn't permit me to refuse care to the monster, but you don't have to do anything. You know that, don't you?"

"I know."

"Chemically, it's almost identical to sodium benzoate—the food preservative. You can buy some of that down at the local co-op. It's easy to mix up the bottles. You'd have to be careful. If you confused them, she would suffer—a lot. Before the end, that is."

"I understand."

Emma put the bottle down. She heard The Dowager calling for her, and she went to the alien, the daughter of many queens, and did as she was told. This time, however, she felt a curious mingling of power and guilt. The Dowager's barbed words and occasional menacing posture were feeble. Emma thought about what the doctor had said, and there was a division and a dispute within herself.

At the thronged co-op the next day, Emma looked at

a clear bottle of sodium benzoate in solution. The bottle
was as cool and impersonal as the paperwork she'd
had to fill out, putting herself on the list for another job
assignment in six to eighteen months. But when Emma
reached for it, her throat tightened and something in the
pit of her stomach turned to hot lead. She turned deliberately away from the preservative. She knew she would not
come back.

There were pustules now, swelling out agonizingly
from all the tender places on The Dowager's body. The
sores stank, deep blue with alien blood, and looked as
if they would burst at the slightest touch. Once, when
Emma accidentally brushed their surface, The Dowager
had stiffened and given out a faint moan. The sound
haunted her human servant more than a thousand harsh
words had ever done.

Emma sprayed The Dowager's eyes and ears with the
clear fluid, letting the sensitive tissues there absorb the
medicine into the elderly alien's bloodstream. In minutes,
The Dowager's body relaxed, free of most of its pain, and
Emma knew the creature's posture well enough that
she understood everything. The Dowager was grateful,
embarrassed at herself, and afraid. After a moment's
reflection, Emma realized: *She's afraid I'll leave her alone
with her pain.*

"I've got some things in my pack," Emma said,
moving away to preserve the alien's dignity. "With your
permission, I could stay in the vesting chamber. Just in
case you wish my services."

"...Yes, human girl. You have my permission. But do
not be noisy, as you always are."

"I won't."

Weeks had passed, and today The Dowager could not speak to Emma. She did not lack the strength in her body; she simply had no words. This morning The Dowager lay on her dais in a mess of her own bodily wastes

The conquerors had called it an act of war any time a human had dared to lay bare hands on their persons without permission to touch that sovereign flesh. Emma had not bothered to ask any permission. The division inside Emma was strong now; old resentment battling new pity. Power fed the one and starved the other, and each new day Emma hoped that The Dowager could not see her biting back the urge to hurt her a little in retaliation for years of scorn.

The Dowager had learned a great deal about human body language as well. She saw more than Emma hoped, but like Emma, she had begun to choose silence and to hope for silence in return.

And so Emma did not humiliate The Dowager with any words at all, but cleaned away the filth, bathing the alien's failing skin, and wiping gently at The Dowager's cloaca. She didn't say the words she had thought a thousand times: *At least my vagina, urethra, and anus are three different organs, superior creature.*

Finally, Emma had no choice but to speak. The Dowager's species did not diaper their young, who took care of themselves from spawning onward. She wanted the alien to understand what she was about to do.

"It will be better if I put something around you, to help you be more comfortable," Emma began to say.

"Do it," said The Dowager.

Please, Emma thought. *Say please.* She thought of the sodium benzoate, of the isolation. Of a thousand insults, but not one of them an ankusha's agony. Not one of them a Scar on her mind or body. Not one of them a woman torturing another living creature with false medicine.

Disgusted at herself for even thinking of such things,

Emma excused herself and took the mess away to dispose
of it.

The news on the visuport had talked of far away
things. Somewhere in the stars the invaders had met a
more powerful culture and were fighting them, desperately. The information was still censored, even nowadays,
but there were ominous implications that humanity
might do well to think about helping the devil it knew.
All of it washed over Emma without much effect. She
had nothing to do with important things. She was just a
xenocare specialist.

The Dowager had not been able to move from her
dais in a long while. Breathing was an effort, even with
fresh air gills implanted (as they had been since her
spawning), and the third lobe of each of her pupils was
lazy and mostly dilated. Emma could barely keep the
alien fed now, and they had not argued in weeks. The
bottle of medicine was almost empty.

"What is your death custom?" The Dowager asked.

"We...we don't really have one," Emma replied. "A lot
of us aren't actually awake for our deaths; not if we can
help it. One of our doctors once said, 'Humans die doped.'
I think he was right."

"That cannot always have been true."

"No. I'm sure it wasn't."

"Then what did you do before you 'died doped'?"

Emma struggled with the question. Humans had
reached the same levels of apparent unity in a lot of areas
The Dowager's species had attained: Monotheism, global
government and economy, and much more. But their
gut-level beliefs, the irrational ones, were still as divided
as ever. Emma felt as billions of others did, considering
herself "spiritual, but not religious." Vague. Shapeless.
What did that mean in the face of something real and

immediate? Death didn't call for "maybe" or "I think." Death would decide matters for you, even if you had no opinion one way or another.

"I don't know if I can speak for everyone."

"Speak for yourself," The Dowager snapped with sudden energy.

Anger flared in Emma. For a moment, she thought of telling The Dowager all the things that had settled in her stomach like sediment over these long years. *Speak for myself! All right, monster, I'll speak for myself and all my people. You're a failure! A loathsome reptilian thing that thinks it still rules my planet, and you have no manners, no culture worth knowing, no love, no charity! You're brutal and nasty and full of self-pity. You condescend to my species, when we have thousands of years of vibrant civilization! How dare you?! How dare you set foot on my planet, old monster!*

Emma trembled with the anger that swept over her, and for a moment she could feel her pulse in her temples. But when she looked down at The Dowager, she saw the pitiful old alien clearly once again.

The Dowager's plated skin, crumbling away in thin, sad layers. Her thick rings of fat sagged and dwindled, as if some invisible spirit had borne away handfuls of her life with every passing hour. The Dowager's complex mouth desperately moistening and re-moistening, her large eyes dilating with an emotion that must have tortured her. The Dowager was afraid to die, especially to die alone, away from all her people. There was no one but Emma to comfort her, and though The Dowager was annoying, impossible, bigoted, thoughtless...within those eyes was another intelligence in the universe, strange and foreign, beginning to drift away from life.

The human woman took a breath.

"All right," Emma said. "I will speak and act for myself."

She reached down for The Dowager's clawed extremity. At first the alien feebly tugged it away, momentarily resuming her normal stature. But after a moment, The Dowager let Emma reach for her, and the human woman laced her fingers between the clawed digits. She had served The Dowager for fifteen years. The old alien, proud descendant of the conquering horde, had never once permitted Emma to directly touch her bare skin. The Dowager felt faintly warm, very dry, and crinkled under Emma's fingers, like dull, old wood shavings.

Emma knelt down by The Dowager's bed and said, "This is a prayer my mother taught me. I don't really believe in it, but it's something."

"Say your prayer."

Emma said it. The words still meant nothing to her, just as the old pictures of steeples and resurrected men had never touched her, but the feeling behind the words spoke to her. She felt the sense, as she always had, that life was enfolded in something larger and wiser, a true meaning behind the existential void. It was probably an illusion, she knew. She saw no reason why truth was best if truth was only pain.

"These are silly words," said The Dowager. "Your species...so absurd." But she let her claws rest intertwined with Emma's fingers.

Emma found herself smiling. "Yes. We are absurd. Very contradictory, as you always say."

"I am always right," The Dowager said, nodding to herself.

"Of course, Dowager," said Emma.

A spasm of pain coiled through The Dowager for a moment, despite her medication. Her breath came in short hisses for several minutes, and her frail digits squeezed tight against Emma's hand. The human made gentle, soothing noises at the alien, gazing upon her with a sad sympathy. When The Dowager focused again, she had the eyes of a swimmer floating above a great abyss.

"Human girl," said The Dowager. "Will you remember

me?"

"Yes."

Alien ears receded into their spaces in The Dowager's skull. A sign Emma had learned to read long ago: *Apprehension. Fear. Uncertainty.*

"Stay here with me."

"I will."

"Human girl...Emma. This world is ours by conquest. The Divine has given us your planet because we are best. I am the daughter of many queens....Many queens."

"Of course, Dowager."

The old creature spoke in a small voice, slowly and carefully, conserving her breath. For long minutes, she seemed not to know where she was, and lapsed into her own language. Emma only understood a little bit of it. It seemed The Dowager was speaking to someone who was not there, someone she might have known a long time ago. Then the alien's consciousness cleared, rising from dazed confusion to a clearer bewilderment.

"Why are you still here?"

Emma smiled very gently. "My death custom."

"But I am..."

"Yes. The daughter of many queens." She dabbed away some drool from the corner of the fading Dowager's mouth. "You have much to take pride in."

The Dowager hesitated, looking up at Emma— Emma, who held the power of life and death over her, as she had for many years. The human girl who had listened to her demeaning talk, sat through her tantrums, and put up with all her demands. The Dowager's people had ruled everything there was, and Emma's people, proud humanity, had felt the conquerors' foot on their collective neck. *How...?*

As if sensing the question, Emma stayed steadily beside The Dowager and gave a soft squeeze of her hand. It took a very long time, but The Dowager gently pressed back on Emma's fingers.

There were no more words.

NEW UNION REQUIREMENT

Gwendolynn Thomas

"I'd like to submit an application for a bonded crew member premium."

"Human option?"

"Yes, please."

"Defensive or engineering detail?"

"Uh...both, please."

"Please hold." The agent squished its pinching arm into the control module, pulling a long form onto the holoscreen and angled it toward the customer. "Scan your chip, please."

The patron waved its tentacle above the holoscreen and the form refreshed, half-completed with his captain designation, identification, and policy numbers.

"Start and end dates of the human's contract?" the agent asked, watching the captain struggle to compensate for the tentacle movement, clearly unaccustomed to the higher pressure of a fully aquatic space station. Spaceships were almost all air-inflated, reinforced water-suits an unfortunate necessity for their passengers to reduce the ship's weight for takeoff—hardly a problem for a station constructed in orbit. The agent ignored the captain's struggles, toggling through the form to the next pull-down menu.

"It came aboard last week and it'll disembark in three years at the Omega Colonies, where we will pick up a new human if possible," the captain answered finally, righting itself.

"You'll have to file for a new insurance premium for that trip unless your current human extends its contract."

"I understand." The captain shifted impatiently, its tentacles spreading out to maintain its buoyancy when it began to sink past the edge of the desk.

"Human's name or identification number?" the agent asked, skipping to the next section.

"They have names?" the captain asked, jetting itself upwards again.

"They name everything," the agent replied. "Carbon age of the human?" it asked, standing taller on its small back claws to see over the control module to maintain eye contact with the constantly moving customer.

"I don't know. It's kind of gray-looking."

The agent pinched its mouth sphincter, its small antennae twitching.

"Male or female human?" it asked, its left eyestalk angling up to glance at the patron again. The captain rubbed a sucker over its large head.

"Uh...I haven't asked. They have sexual dimorphism?"

The agent pulled its pinching claw from the control module to push a box of external drives across its desk.

"Might I suggest one of our pamphlets, Captain?" it asked, and the captain's skin slowly shifted pinker.

"No...thank you. Sorry about that."

"You'll have to get back to me with that information before we finalize your take-off permit. Our office contact numbers will be on the front and last page of your insurance contract addendum." The agent ran its grasping claw over the top of the toggle board, scrolling down the form to the next chart titled *Current Bond Designation*. "How long has the human been on the physical premises of the ship?"

"Not just held the contract?" the captain asked, its eye dilating in surprise.

"They bond with the objects in their immediate

area, Captain," the agent replied, not looking away from the holoscreen as it entered a few numbers into the spreadsheet.

"I thought artificial cognizance was still tied up in patent suits. Is human technology so advanced?"

"No. They don't require their bond targets to be sentient."

"At all?" The captain glanced down at the box of pamphlet chips, but did not take one.

"Have you never seen them name a ship? Many humans consider it possible to alter pure-chance reactions negatively to not name them," the agent replied.

"Deep-space zeppelins and whale ships have a certain level of awareness—"

"Irrelevant, Captain. Humans have been observed to name their toasters."

"Their what?"

"Low-tech space heaters for bread. A female human named one Fuzzy, though it was not, and cried when its cord got caught in a laser-peeler drawer."

"That's...madness."

"Your first human, Captain?" the agent asked, scrolling down the spreadsheet again, skipping questions about scent trails and urine marks designed for other species.

"New union requirement," the captain replied. "Is it that obvious?"

"The toaster reaction is quite typical, Captain. It's why we offer the best discounts for human crewed vessels. Human captains have been shown to intentionally die with their ship simply to express their commitment to its survival—that they'd have died for it if it would have helped, so they'll die if it wouldn't."

"With no hope at all? Just...dying?" The captain slowly sank past the edge of the desk again.

"So you can imagine what they'll do if there is hope, Captain. Humans asphyxiate while occupied fitting their offspring or invalids with breath masks so often that human air suits play a reminder to secure their own masks before assisting others on repeat until their oxygen levels are stabilized."

"Olaf's ovipositors!" The captain jetted upward.

"Language, Captain, please!" the agent exclaimed, its eyestalks straightening to glare at the client. The captain's skin rippled with displeasure, shifting blue.

"Apologies," it replied gruffly and squirted back from the desk.

"Class 4 human bonds—including consistent physical contact, shared battle experience, or offspring, have an eighty-two percent success rate for self-sacrificial actions. They're like sentient doliolids," the agent explained, returning to its usual monotone.

"Are they hive-minded?" the captain asked, subdued.

"Sort of. Most of their reactions are determined by a colony of gut bacteria operating within a tube beneath their stomach, but each single human body thinks of itself as an individual mind without influence," the agent replied, pushing the bowl of pamphlets a little closer to the captain.

"They're just...bacteria in a tube in a meat suit? But... how did they get into space?"

"A few more questions, please, to determine the estimated class of pack bond your human will acquire. Has it made physical contact of any nonviolent sort with any of your crew?" the agent asked, ignoring the question.

"No."

"Engaged in battle or endured any high-death-probability situations alongside any member of your crew?"

"We're a transport vessel..." the captain murmured.

"Please answer the questions directly," the agent replied, its eyes focused on the different charts it scrolled past.

"No."

"Has it ever eaten food from the serving of another

crew member?"

"My first mate gave it a cricket cup once, but the human tossed it out half-eaten later," the captain replied, wrapping one of its tentacles around the desk leg to pull itself closer.

"Only the one time?"

"Yes."

"All right. One point there then…" the agent murmured, its claw squeezing at the toggles until the holoscreen switched to another form. "Has it shown copulation interest in any of your crew?"

"We're mostly cephaloids."

"I…see." The agent flicked an eyestalk at the captain and glanced away.

"Any relatives of the human on board?" it asked.

"Still cephaloids…" the captain drawled.

"Please answer the questions directly. Does it refer to any of the crew by shortened, disfigured, or unassigned designation names or labels?"

"It calls my first mate O Captain Puffy, My Puffy."

"Does it show any affinity toward them?"

"As a reproductive mate?"

"For example," the agent replied, pulling open the desk drawer and digging inside it with two of its side legs until it hauled out a memo stone to shove across the coral desk. "Does your human show any of these signs of courtship for allies or mating partners?"

The cephaloid captain jerked closer to the memo stone in a short burst from its muscular siphon and clipped its beak against the hard table top. It backed up, pink again.

"Does it continually seek out an individual crew member with which to complain about the other crew members?" the captain read aloud, glancing up at the agent as if to check that the memo stone was not a prank. The agent stared back, waiting for an answer.

"How would I know that? Wouldn't it be complaining

about me?"

"It's important to keep tabs on the conversation of your human crew members for insurance purposes, Captain. Most human bonding rituals occur in spoken dialogue," the agent replied seriously. The captain returned to the memo stone.

"Does it directly insult another crew member without any expectation that the crew member will be insulted? What does that mean?" the captain asked and the agent closed the desk drawer with a loud bang.

"We get that question every time. Skip that one. It's probably a misprint," it replied and the captain's eye glanced back at the memo.

"No. None of these. Still...it's possible a mating interest may develop. Can I update the premium if that occurs?" the captain asked, getting redder.

"Yes, certainly. We can prorate any options you take from the date of copulation," the agent replied, toggling the answers into the spreadsheet. It looked up finally and pulled a new chart up onto the holoscreen. "Optimum Insurance can only offer you a Class 1 Bonding Designation—which offers no premium benefits for the first three weeks."

"None? But the human costs 1,300,000 pezel credits a month!" the captain protested, ink bulging in its side sacks and painting its front black.

"You could delay your insurance benefits until the thirtieth," the agent suggested, its grasping claw hovering over the toggle board. "After that point, there will be a graduated benefit plan which can be upgraded at any evidence of increased emotional ties."

"Impossible! We enter deep space on Friday. This is why unions should not have a say in hiring decisions!" the captain growled, its serrated beak flashing in the low-fusion light. The insurance agent ignored its complaint and skittered across the hard floor to the other side of the small office to unlock one of the filing cabinets lining the back wall.

"A class three designation will take an extra 600,000 pezels off your monthly premium, if you'd like to try to upgrade your human integration program," it said, extracting a few data chips from the drawer, delicately clamped in its pinching claw, and making its way back toward its desk, dodging the fake kelp plant in the corner. It pushed the chips into the control module and pulled up a sample insurance addendum.

"That doesn't even cover the cost of the human's contract!" the captain protested.

"It is the best we can offer, captain. A new human does not offer increased ship protection until after that initial bonding period is complete," it ordered and the captain pulled a sucker over its head again.

"What does a class two bond require?"

"If I may, Captain, we offer multiple human integration programs."

"Well, the contract is already signed. Might as well throw good money after bad."

"Humans can be invaluable, Captain. There's no alien you'd want more in a crisis. For the quickest bonding experience I would suggest you arrange a battle in which the human takes a decisive action to the benefit of its crew—they can bond by habit on occasion—and what they've done once they're likely to repeat," the agent replied calmly, pulling a brochure up on the holoscreen. A video hologram of a human pulling a group of promons from a burning engine room played on repeat.

"We're a transport vessel traveling between two of the most regulated black hole ports in the known universe. It's not likely," the captain commented dryly.

"May I suggest your ship gets hit by an oddly-un-traceable asteroid and requires a dangerous repair mission to save the life of everyone on board, to which your human is randomly assigned if it does not volunteer? We offer the full program on CDEcho-three and

sixteen li'years off Andromeda, both on your way. The
Adamantium Package includes a publicity bulletin sent
to other humans to reinforce the hero self-image of your
human. That will earn you six points and you can get
a discount on your security premium, as the package
includes certification in hull-breach alarm responses
if you buy within twenty four hours of registering for
Optimum Insurance. With four more points it would pay
for itself."

The captain groaned.

"We can offer you a class four bonding option,
which will take 1,200,000 pezels off your premium," the
agent announced, switching the hologram to another
display of charts. The captain's ink sacks began to drain,
returning it to its natural green color. "Just make sure it
has reached a class two bond before the program's start
date."

"All right. What do I have to do?" the captain asked,
its tentacles dangling limply.

"Humans will do most of their pack bonding left to
their own devices, but there are tried-and-true ways to
speed the process up. Will it eat with your crew or on its
own?" the agent asked, pushing away from the control
module to focus on the captain again.

"At the same shift designation or—"

"Physical premises, captain. The closer the better, up
to a distance of one half human arm-length measured
from the shoulder. Beyond that, the human becomes
territorial," the agent answered.

"We'll measure its arms when it comes aboard," the
captain promised and the agent nodded swiftly.

"Will it be sleeping with or near any of the crew?"

"...Yes?" the captain guessed and the agent clicked
its pinchers together in a slow applause. The captain
reached out a tentacle to take a pamphlet chip from the
offered bowl. The agent bobbed its eyestalks, pleased, and
the captain quietly pulled another chip from the bowl.

"For my first mate," it murmured.

"O Captain Puffy, My Puffy," the agent commented dryly, pushing its pincher back into the control module with a squelch. "So the human will join the transport ship expecting a pleasant, safe journey across the galaxy with its luggage. Adversity can be quite bonding; captains often arrange for luggage and room tickets to be misplaced for up to three days, forcing a small group of humans to suffer without their effects together. The results are quite promising," the agent related, dragging the displaced bowl of external drives back to its spot.

"All right. It'll lose its luggage and spend three days on a bed net in the air deck. I have a few promon aboard; they can join it," the captain agreed easily, pulling a seaweed roll and pen from its satchel. It unrolled the seaweed to an empty page and began scratching notes.

"Excellent. Make sure the human works near those promon, with an air-voice translator. Is O Captain Puffy, My Puffy very furred?"

"Excuse me?" the captain asked and the agent waved its small grasping claw, dismissing the protest.

"Humans will bond and initiate physical contact with strangers proportionate to the length of carotin in their skin follicles," the agent explained.

"Fuzziness?" the captain asked and the agent bobbed its eyestalks again. "Uh...yes, O Captain—That is...my first mate is fuzzy."

"Excellent. You said you were applying for engineering detail?" the agent asked.

The captain waved a tentacle back and forth indecisively, its skin undulating again. "What precisely does that mean?" it asked and the agent let out a heavy release of bubbles.

"Humans are incredibly innovative, Captain. It's a direct result of their insanity. If your human has been educated in deep space communications or electromagnetic propulsion systems, you will be able to register for a research grant for any travel expenses beyond 2,000,000 li'years from charted space. Optimum Insurance has allied with the Federation's programs in research and development and we offer a two-month free premium for that same sector, covering up to 200,000,000 pezel credits of property damage and 1,000,000 pezel credits of life insurance."

"That's a worthless amount of life insurance," the captain complained.

"It won't be needed, Captain. Not with a human on board."

"Why is deep space travel subsidized?"

"Only with a human," the agent insisted.

"Because they self-sacrifice?"

"No, Captain. Because if anything goes wrong, your human will get you home. And your human will get you home in an entirely new way."

"They're bacteria in a meat suit!" the captain exclaimed, flapping its front tentacles erratically.

"They breathe a flammable gas and contain some of alien life's strongest acids in their stomach. They eat asteroids, Captain, and they mapped tetraquarks before their first extraspecies contact. Don't underestimate them. This is a species that visited its moon before developing external computation with no intent to gather any consumable resources there. Nothing but a few chunks of it to 'prove they'd done it'—seemingly to themselves. Your human will get you where you're going. Are you interested in taking advantage of the scenic route to the Omega Colonies?"

"Free insurance, you said?" the captain asked, slowly rising toward the top of the room.

"For two months, Captain. And that grant includes fuel."

"Oh, eggsacks. It's the only way we'll turn a profit with these requirements," the captain admitted, turning to squish itself back toward the floor. "With these insurance options every idiot and their ectoplasm will be traveling through deep space, keel-hauling their token human."

"It'll mark a revolution in space exploration. Your human might be the first alien to discover inorganic life!" the agent replied, waving its claws in enthusiasm.

"And by the sound of it, it'll proceed to hug it to death," the captain growled.

"Inorganic life is very unlikely to be fuzzy in any way," the agent protested, and the captain groaned. "Their curiosity is valuable, Captain. It could save your life."

"I'm a transport vessel captain!" it repeated, throwing its tentacles up around its beak again.

"You're going into deep space, now," the agent pointed out, scratching at the back of its carapace with its large pinching claw.

"Because of the flopping human!" the captain shouted, and the agent bobbed its eyestalks.

"A fair complaint, Captain, but you'll have to take that up with the Federation lobbyists and your union," it pointed out.

"All right, the full package, please. I'll get it eating and sleeping and renaming my crew by the time we reach Andromeda, and then we can scare it half to death with a fake asteroid before we head toward deep space to actually die without assistance or recourse," the captain agreed, slumping.

"Ink here, please. And here, and date it here with your registration number and take-off date," the agent replied, swiftly pulling the long form back onto the holoscreen.

THE SOUND OF HIS FOOTSTEPS

Mariah Southworth

I don't think I will ever forget the sound his footsteps made on that hostile world.

Crunch CRACK crunch.

The sun beat down through the cloth of his shirt. Hot and uncomfortable, I huddled beneath the material. Whatever my discomfort, it was better than direct exposure to the harsh, unforgiving rays of the sun. I thought, briefly, of him, knowing him to be one of the paler breeds of his species, without even the dubious protection of melanin to shield him from the sun's radiation.

I wondered if he burned so that I could be protected.

Crunch SNAP crack.

Oh, Merciful Mother, it hurt, it hurt so much.

Crunch CRACK crunch.

I opened my eyes, and everything was yellow, colored by the material of his shirt. From my position I could see a glimpse of the ground—dark gray plates of slate, like a pile of fish scales. I saw them shift and crack each time his boot came down on them.

How many miles could he carry me, underneath the sun, over the hot slate?

I closed my eyes and I thought of you, Salaseal. I thought of happier days, before we went careening out over the galaxies, away to that awful planet.

"You're sending a *what*?" I asked, unable to believe what Salaseal had said. She turned from the clear glass of her tower wall, and the light of the green moon slid over her opalescent skin. "I am sending a human on the expedition," she repeated, her voice calm and matter-of-fact.

I shook my head, still unwilling to believe that she would be so stupid. Salaseal was educated, after all—one of the finest scientists to ever come from the Halls of Silq.

"Sal," I said exasperatedly. "Sal, you can't be serious. They're violent animals. They wiped out life on their entire planet, for Mother's sake!"

"Ciliaso," she sighed, reverting to the childhood version of my name. "That was ages ago, and the humans that we have in the Collective were not the ones responsible for that."

"They're the descendants of the ones responsible," I persisted.

"They're the descendants of the ones that the Red Queen decided to save," she retorted, the decorative, feminine fins on her head waving back and forth, as they did when she was annoyed.

"They still have those violent tendencies; you know that."

She sighed at me and looked back out through the glass at the fungal forest below. The green moon cast everything in a soft light, muting the vibrant color of the mushroom trees, blending together the shadows of the climbing molds and decorative truffles. A breeze stirred, sending a cloud of spores to drift sedately over the monochromatic landscape. On the horizon, I saw the pale sliver of the white moon as it ponderously began its month-long journey across the night sky.

"Yes, Liaso," she said. "Humans have a great capacity for violence. They also have one of the greatest capacities for love, empathy, loyalty, creativity...I could go on!" She turned away from the window again, this time crossing the room and draping herself over her carved shell divan

"They are extremists," she continued, looking at me with serious, dark eyes. "They are survivors. Three expeditions have gone before us to this planet—all of them have failed, and only one of them had a crew member return alive. You remember Drog, the Ursoid mercenary?"

I winced, remembering. Drog had not lived long in the satellite hospital he had been admitted to.

"The human is coming on this expedition," she concluded. "We *will* bring back the flucurial, and we will use it to stop the plague on Hapsoid. I would build the entire crew of humans if I thought that the company would allow it." She tilted her head, her expression lightening. "What's the matter, anyway, you think your cultured sensibilities can't stand a few months in the company of a barbarian?"

Crunch crunch SNAP

I missed my home. I missed the cool light of the green moon, the warm damp of the fungal forests. I missed the welcoming eyes of my family's pet armor bug, and the smell of sporeing season.

"You doing okay, Lia?" The human's harsh voice startled me from my misery.

My speech organs were so dry, it was hard to say anything for a moment. "No," I rasped, wincing at the sound of my own voice.

"Ah, it'll be fine," he said.

If I could have spared the energy, I would have thrashed my mouth tentacles in surprise. "How can you say that?" I asked. "We alone survived the explosion! I've lost...I've lost..." My stomach rolled queasily at the thought. "We have no supplies," I continued, "no ship, no communications..." I wanted to say more, but I could not. My mind was still too shaken to fully wrap around the horror we had been through.

"You're still alive," the human pointed out. "I'm in good shape, and hey, maybe we *will* find this magic cure-all that the Lady Sah-le-seel was so keen to get."

Salaseal, if you could have heard how he pronounced your name... "I suppose I must admire your stubborn delusions of hope," I muttered.

He laughed—that barking sound he always makes when amused, so like the sound that mating ocean-cats make. "I think that's the nicest thing you ever said to me, Lia."

Perhaps he was right. I remember the first thing I thought when I saw him.

Oh god, he's got metal in his face.

That wasn't the most jarring thing about the human—they are, after all, most unlovely creatures—but it was the first thing my eyes were drawn to. The polished metal stud glinted from its place in the human's right ear, eye catching both by its shine and the brutal implications it held.

I wasn't the only one interested in the piece of metal, but unlike my fellow Silvasian and the slender, bird-like Eatherla who gathered around the creature, *I* didn't intend to lavish attention on him for his self-harm.

"Did you grow it?" asked the young Silvasian, leaning in so close his suckered mouth arms nearly touched the human's face.

"No, no," trilled the Eatherla, eyes shining with admiration, "it is a wound that he decorated. We have the practice among my people. It is considered a sign of great courage and virility."

"Uh, well," the human said, his mouth edges turning upwards, "you're probably closest Skee; it's just a piercing."

The Eatherla's feathered crest rose in confusion. "I do

not understand," she admitted. "Is that not what I said?"

"He means he did it himself," I interrupted, unwilling to watch the farce any longer. "He punched a hole in his ear and put a piece of metal into it to keep it from closing."

The young adventurers looked at me in disbelief, then turned their shocked gazes onto the human.

The human, rather than having the sense to be embarrassed for his barbarism and wanton disregard for his own health, just nodded his head. "Right," he said.

Crunch.

The rhythm of the human's walking stopped; I thought it never would. He had been walking for hours, far longer than I would have imagined him capable of. I opened my eyes and, to my terror, saw a glimpse of green beneath me.

"What are you doing?" I gasped, only to shudder in pain as he removed the shirt from my back, jostling my terrible wound.

"Setting you down," he said with a sigh, placing me on the deceptively fine and soft grass. "The sun's just about down, and we should stop for the night."

Despite my fear, I was alarmed to hear of the time. "You walked for the entire day?" I asked. I must have slept without realizing it. "Did you stop?"

"I was only walking," the human said.

Aghast, I looked at our surroundings. The green veldt was like the one that we had landed on. It was elevated ground, and from atop it I could see the slate flat the human had walked across. It was so vast I couldn't see the end, couldn't see where we had landed.

That brought back the severity of our current situation. "We can't stay on the grass!" I protested. "Not after what happened."

The human sat down next to me, and I finally looked at him. "Your skin!" I exclaimed. What had been as pale as the flesh of a suede mushroom at the beginning of the journey had turned a bright and startling pink. It was especially bad over the curve of his shoulders, where the skin had gone tight and angry, but looking at his face, I could see that all the high points were kissed with red. "Radiation burns," I said, feeling sick with sudden guilt. I had been afraid of what would happen without his shirt to protect him.

The human looked at his shoulder, then back at me. He shrugged, and I saw him wince. "I've had worse," he said. "It's just a sunburn."

I remembered hearing tales of radiation burn victims. A burn so bad that it changed their skin color and had put them in the hospital for days. The human, quite literally, shrugged it off.

I didn't know what to say to his callousness. He said nothing about my silence, probably taking it for fatigue. Looking away from me, he unclipped the bottle from his belt. He took a small sip, then offered it to me.

The scent of water nearly drove me mad. I clasped the bottle in my suckered face arms and guzzled the sweet, life giving water, unable to think of anything else. It wasn't until the bottle was nearly empty that I realized just how much I had drunk.

"You did not drink enough," I accused as he took the bottle back.

He shrugged again, despite his burn. "I know you cuttle-fish guys need more water than we do." He must have successfully read my dubious look, because he continued rather defensively. "I kept a rock in my mouth, it's fine."

"A rock?" I asked, confused.

"Sure," he said, pulling the pebble in question from his pocket. "It's an old marching trick I read about. You keep a rock in your mouth, and it makes you salivate, and you don't feel as thirsty." He finished the rest of the water in one quick swallow, oblivious to my shock.

I closed my eyes. It was too much. I was injured, probably delirious, and the human got more and more bizarre the more time I spent with him.

It was a sign of my illness that I didn't remember our danger until then.

"The grass," I said weakly. "We must get off of it."

"And what, spend the night down on the slate?" He shook his head. "No way—you remember the weather reports of this planet. We're staying on the high ground." He stood up with a grunt and picked me up, careful of my wound. I finally saw what lay waiting behind us. "See?" he said. "I found a cave for shelter and everything. The universe provides, little friend."

A barbarian to the end.

"What is *that*?" I sneered, coming unannounced into the recreation room of the ship. The human looked up at me, making one of his unreadable faces.

He knew what I was talking about—he couldn't play dumb this time. He raised the shinning bit of metal he had been playing with. "It's a machete," he said. "I'm making a new grip for it."

My mouth arms curled in disdain. "Why?"

The furry little ridges on his face went up. "Well, it's not like I don't have the time—you must admit, things get boring on the ship."

"No, no," I said, continuing to sneer, "I mean why would you bring such a primitive thing? We gave you a blaster, didn't we? Isn't that enough weaponry to satisfy you?"

The furry ridges went down again. "Blaster won't do much against the plant life," he grunted, half turning away from me.

I trilled my derision at him.

Even the human needed *some* sleep, and as it got dark, he finally drifted off into slumber. I lay awake a little longer, the cold of the cave floor contrasting with the heat from his body. My stump throbbed painfully, and the horror of the missing limb gnawed at my gut.

Why was he helping me? I had never been kind to him, he had no reason to bond with me. This human couldn't possibly think of me as a friend, and I certainly wasn't blood related to him. He had no *reason* to save me, to carry me those many miles, to give me his water. Merciful Mother, I didn't even *look* like him, not like the Eatherla did, with her two legs and two eyes.

Maybe it was a normal human reaction, though. *The universe's orphans*, that's what they called them in school, remember? Always so willing to adopt anyone into their "family."

I finally dropped to sleep just as the rain started. I don't remember if I dreamed.

I awoke to a crooning sound. The pain in my limb throbbed, keeping me from focusing. Finally, I realized that the human was making the noise. "What is that?" I rasped, wincing at the weakness in my voice. The sound stopped.

"I was just singing a lullaby," the human said. "My voice isn't as pretty as Skee's, I know, but..." he trailed off.

Singing. He used his same speech organs for singing! If I could have laughed I would have, but I didn't have the energy. "Was that your first language?" I asked.

"Yeah," he replied. "And the song's all the way from Earth."

Did he sound sad? I would be if I knew my planet was dead, dead by the hand of my own species, no less. It made me feel oddly close to the human, that sympathy.

"Want to know what it means?" he asked.

I didn't, but I didn't have the energy to speak anymore, so he told me anyways.

"It's about the singer's son," he explained, "who goes far away from home and dies before he gets back."

Utterly morbid, but I expected no less from a human.

"Let me see if I can translate it," he said. "Um, Oh Danny-child, the uh, the flutes the flutes are beckoning, from field to field and down the mountainside..." He broke off into a hum. "Not quite the same," he sighed.

I felt him sit up behind me, and only with the sudden cold did I realize how much warmth his body had given me.

"Sound's like the rain stopped," he said.

He was right, the rain had stopped, and it left the world transformed. The slate basin we had walked in the day before had been filled to the brim with water. It lapped at the edge of the sinister grass, and I was suddenly, unashamedly grateful that the human had made us sleep on high ground.

The human was unfazed by how close we had come to drowning. "Here's a bit of luck," he said, setting me down and filling the bottle. He drank, then drank again, then filled the bottle so I could drink. Then he filled the bottle a third time, buckled it to his belt, picked me up, and set off over the grass without further comment.

"You don't seem quite so chipper this morning," he said after a while.

I took my time in answering him. The water had revitalized me, but not by much. "I am dying," I said simply.

"Ah, Lia, you're not dying."

"I have lost too much blood, and my primary limb is gone." I was too tired to sound irritated at his blind hope. "I am going to die out here, just like the rest of the crew. Just like everyone who came before us."

The human was silent for a while, and I thought maybe I had finally made a dent in that unbreakable optimism of his. The thought made me inexplicably sad.

"It *is* weird that we haven't found any of those ships," he muttered. "They all landed near here." Then, louder, he continued. "This flutewhatsit that we're supposed to find..."

"Flucurial," I corrected.

"Right that. It's supposed to be a cure-all. If we find it, will you live?"

"I don't know," I sighed. "No one's found any in centuries. Most of its properties are probably exaggerated."

"It's supposed to cure that plague though, right?"

I thought of the images from Hapsoid and nearly lost the water in my stomach. Living tissue rotting, blood running from eyes like tears, children with their entire faces fallen away...

"Yes," I said weakly. "It is their only hope." Did he grasp the importance of our mission? Did he know about flucurial, that it had been used up before synthesizer technology had become advanced enough to replicate it? He knew that we had gotten reports of it from the first exploration to this planet, and he knew those scientists and their ship had been destroyed before they could send any of the precious substance home, but did he *care*?

When I died, would he go on to find the flucurial on the off-chance that he would be rescued? I didn't know, couldn't know, how his alien mind worked.

I thought of that first doomed crew. What had killed them? The harsh sun, the unpredictable weather? The exploding grass? The vicious, carnivorous plant life that had taken out the Ursoid crew?

What would kill us?

The sound of the human's footsteps was different on the grass. Muffled, soft. I could only hope that his tread was light enough that it didn't trigger an explosion.

"Don't land in the slate," I directed, looking through the window of the bridge. "That's how the crew sent after the Ursoid Mercenaries died—those slate basins flood."

Obedient, the lizard-alien (I never could pronounce its name, nor that of its species) steered the ship into a perfect landing on the bright, green grass. "Excellent," I said, releasing myself from the suspension seat. All around me, the rest of the crew did the same. Asoi, my fellow Silvasian, Skee the Etherla and her nest-sib, Hak, the lizard-alien, whom everyone had ended up calling Hiss, since that was the noise he made most often.

And the human, of course.

I was looking forward to having some space from him. Three months in a small ship had been quite enough. "Go take that skewer of yours and scout around or something," I said. "Make sure none of those carnivorous plants are around."

His brow ridges furrowed and his mouth edges turned down, but he listened to me. He took his machete and he left. Maybe he was sick of being around me, too.

"Liaso," trilled Hak. "Come and look at these readings."

I went, I looked. They made little sense to me. "You *did* cut the engines, yes?" I asked Hiss. He hissed in reply, nodding slowly.

"Then what is this build-up of heat underneath us?" I asked.

He never got to answer. The next thing I knew there was fire, and the sound of great, booming thunder. I was flung against the unforgiving wall of the ship, then tossed into the air before slamming down hard again. White-hot pain lanced up from my primary limb, and I screamed.

The next thing I remember is the human, soot clinging to his porous, rough face, moisture beading grossly on his forehead. He laid me on the slate without a word. I sat up just in time to see him running back into the inferno of the ship.

He told me later, as he tied the tourniquet around what was left of my primary limb, that something under the ship had exploded, sending it into the air like a child's spinning top. Most of it had crashed, thankfully, onto the slope of slate, and not back on the grass. The impact of the pieces that *did* fall onto the grass caused more explosions, tossing them into the air again and again, until the pieces were too small to create enough force to explode further.

Hiss had been one of those pieces.

Hak had been impaled by a broken pipe.

Skee had died upon impact.

Asoi had succumbed to his burns within the first minute.

It was just me and the human left in the hostile wasteland.

My wound didn't really hurt anymore. I felt cold. I didn't even notice when we stopped.

"Damn," the human muttered.

He lifted me, and I forced my eyes to focus. We had come to a sheer rock face the color of the orange gills of the fleece mushrooms back home. The color of the rare red moon. The color of the hair that grows in patches on the human's body.

"It's the cliffs from the first reports," I heard myself sigh. "The flucurial is supposed to be on top of them."

The human never even questioned climbing the cliffs. He had already committed.

I was the problem.

"I'm going to need my hands," the human said. "Can you cling to my neck?"

I tried, I really did, but my secondary limbs had gone numb, and I could not grip with them.

"I'm dying," I told the human again. I felt very calm

about it, a mental defense mechanism, no doubt. Still,
I thought I had to convince the human to go after the
flucurial. "Salaseal will do a flyby in a month's time if she
does not hear from us. Get the flucurial, please."

He looked at me for a long time. I had always hated
his pale eyes. I know that there are humans who have
darker eyes, and had often wondered why you had
assigned one of the uglier humans to the crew. Strangely
enough, in that moment, I *didn't* hate his eyes.

"I'm going to get you that flucurial," he told me, "and
I'm going to bring it back to you, and you're going to be
fine."

I didn't believe him, but I didn't say it.

He found a hole in the cliff to leave me in. He insisted
on leaving his blaster with me, even though we both
knew that he would be facing those carnivorous plants
on top of the cliff. He had his machete—that hunk of
sharpened metal that I had berated him for so many
times.

He started climbing. I drifted in and out of
consciousness.

I found myself back in the Halls of Silq, back in my
very first year. The other children sat around me, listening to our lecturer.

"Fela-qui, also known as the Red Queen, is one of
the more well-known of the Cloud Race, famous for her
habits of going to dying planets and collecting samples of
the life about to be wiped out. Her vast artificial satellites
are her living monument, where her collections of extinct
species can still be viewed by the public."

"Lecturer?"

I glanced to my left, recognizing the voice. I saw *you*
Salaseal, as you were then; your little fins underdevel-
oped, waiting for puberty to make them glorious, your

skin the pale blue of childhood. I never told you, but I had quite the crush on you back then. Maybe you knew.

"Yes Sosalaseal?" said the lecturer.

"Is it true that the Red Queen saved the humans?"

"Yes, Sosalaseal, she did. The humans remain the only sentient species that the Red Queen saved."

"So that's who we have to blame," I muttered under my breath. Sosalaseal shot me a look. I kept quiet, but I didn't need to say anything. Liseosa said it for me.

"My mother says that humans are no good," she piped up. "They just sit around in the satellite ghettos doing horrid things to each other, and when they get a spaceship, they just turn into bandits."

"Don't speak out of turn, Liseosa," the lecturer scolded, but it was too late, the class had gotten excited.

"Nothing kills them," I added. "And they breed like crazy. They're like vermin."

Half the class giggled at that. Sosalaseal did not.

"Settle down class, settle down," the Lecturer told us. "You must drink."

What? I wondered.

She looked at me as she said it again. "Drink Lia, please."

Something pressed against my mouth.

"Please don't leave me alone."

It tasted sweet and bitter at the same time. It was almost disgusting, but the moment it touched the inside of my mouth, I felt a wonderful heat run through me. I drank and drank, and the numbness vanished, the pain that had become the backdrop of my reality faded away. Energy tingled through me, and I opened my eyes and saw the human looking at me.

He didn't look well. There was an angry scratch across his sunburned cheek, and his orange hair stuck up in all directions, bits of leaf and vegetation caught in it. His pale eyes were rimmed with red, and green juice had stained the knees of his trousers.

No being had ever looked more lovely.

Then it dawned on me that I was the first person in centuries to taste flucurial. Joy flooded through me, its intensity in direct proportion to the depths of my earlier despair. "Hello," I said, and the human laughed with joy. Even his barking sounded good.

We crossed the grass again, and I no longer feared that our weight would trigger an explosion. We reached the edge of the slate, and I clung to his back as he waded out into the now waist-high water. The sun was not so harsh then, and the flucurial had healed me enough that I actually enjoyed the walk. He taught me how to sing his Danny-child song, and I marveled at the novelty of using my speech organs to sing.

The second time the human crossed the slate took even less time than the first. I dozed off after a while, unable to stay awake as long as he could, and when I awoke I found that we were already back at the wreckage of the ship.

The rain hadn't caused as much damage as we had feared. I directed the human towards fixing the communications. He did well—those nimble fingers of his more than made up for his lack of technical knowledge.

When he finished, he went into the burnt-out husk of the ship and returned with some salvaged foodstuffs. We ate at dusk by the light of the blinking distress signal.

The stars came out. Remembering the star charts, I found my home sun. I glanced over and saw that the human also looked up at the sky. "Do you miss your planet?" I asked him.

He shook his head slowly. "I never knew my planet."

I waved my face tentacles in sympathy. "It must have been quite a terrifying place, to have produced your species."

That made him laugh, and I found that I was coming to enjoy the sound. It had a round, rich feeling to it that was quite comforting.

I fell asleep in his lap, the heat of his body warming me.

I awoke to the sound of a space ship landing.

It was an older model, one of the Void Swimmers from the Silver Satellite. The human stood as it landed on the slate field, carrying me with him. I was relieved to see the ship—I hadn't been looking forward to even another day on that dreadful planet. The door of the ship opened, and out came a small group. They approached us, and I realized that they were also humans. Then, with a sinking feeling, I realized *all* of the crew was human.

They did not speak Collective. Instead, they spoke the language that the Danny-child song was in. They spoke to each other, then they spoke to my human.

"What are they saying?" I asked. I could feel my human's tension as he held me, heard the increased beat of his heart.

"Shh," he hushed me, and one of the other humans pointed to me and said something harsh, I don't know what.

It all happened very fast after that. One moment my human held me close, the next I was falling to the ground. I didn't get to see much of the fight, because I tumbled over the slight incline of the slate, and by the time I managed to catch myself on my secondary limbs, one human already lay dead, a smoking blaster hole in his chest.

I don't think I realized how much I had come to care for my human until I saw the dead one. I thought that maybe it was him, and that made me feel sick with dread. But it was not him, he still fought the other humans, trading blaster shot for blaster shot. I watched, fascinated and horrified, as he gunned down another of his fellow species, then, when he ran out of charges, he threw the gun at the third one's head, dropping him like a sack of rocks. The last enemy human blasted my human in the shoulder and I cried aloud in rage and anguish.

Sensing victory, the enemy human charged, but he had not realized that my human carried a machete. The enemy's life ended violently and painfully, bleeding his red blood out onto the slate.

Breathing heavily, my human returned to me, and he picked me up, those killer hands holding me carefully, asking if I was okay, apologizing for dropping me. How very strange, that he could hold me so gently after being so brutal.

The rest is self evident. We took the bandit's ship. They had been using the planet as a scavenging ground for some time, returning every so often to retrieve the scrap left by the exploding grass. My human told me they had admitted to killing the first ship of scientists.

So that is the tale, dear Salaseal. I don't know what I learned from it. I mean, I *was* right; humans are violent, cruel beings. Those bandits killed for scrap money, and my human killed them just as easily. Then again, *you* were also right. I wouldn't be alive today if you hadn't insisted on sending a human with us.

I don't know if I learned a lesson or not, but I did gain a friend.

I hope that the synthesizing is going well, and I look forward to seeing you again on the moon of Hapsoid, when we finally stop the plague.

Your dearest friend,

Liaso.

P.S. Yes, I did finally ask the human his name. It's Frank. I don't think I will ever be able to pronounce it.

NO WAY THIS COULD GO WRONG

Alex Pearl

Dyson Field Consortium Station, Apartment District

Stars flickered behind Nines' face as Maz watched her on the apartment monitor, searching her girlfriend's features for telltale flickers of emotion. All Maz could tell, despite her concern, was that Nines was waiting for her to continue talking.

"So...That's at eight—the dancing, I mean, and we're all talking about getting drinks before that."

"Okay, awesome!" Nines said, her face bright.

"Yeah," Maz said.

"Everything alright?"

"I don't know," Maz said, twirling a lock of her hair around her finger. "It seems weird doing something like this without you, you know?"

"Not really! You need to get out and have fun, Maz. The station's a great place to try new stuff, whether I'm there or not. Have a few drinks! Have fun dancing! Hell, bring someone home!"

"You know I'm not going to do that!" Maz laughed nervously and flushed red.

"Well you should! Not like I'm gonna get any action here on the beetle barge. You'll need to get enough tail for the both of us."

"Oh, right! How's the ship treating you?" Maz asked. To Maz's discomfort, Nines caught the subject change with a wry smile. She humored Maz regardless.

"You know, things are fine. The adjustment's getting a little easier, but the translator software's still having trouble. Burg's my girl, though, she's doing an awesome job picking up the nuances of Anthrop."

"Do you think the rest of the Grzzh will catch on that quick? On the ship, I mean." Maz felt a twinge of self-consciousness toward the pronunciation of the species' name. The Grrzh's characteristic back-of-the-throat buzz had eluded her since she started consulting as a behaviorist with the embassy, while Nines had picked up the dialect much more readily. If Maz had bungled it, Nines gave no sign.

"What? Oh, no, naw. Burg's an ambassadress, linguistics are just her thing. I doubt that any other Grzzh are gonna be able to figure out how I talk before my tour's finished."

"I'm sorry, sweetheart. But at least you've got her to talk to, right?"

"Yeah, Burg's a treat. Sounds like you've made a few friends on the station, too," Nines said, with an accompanying bounce of her eyebrows. Maz gave a guilty smile and reached for her hair again.

"The work at the embassy's been pretty good for that. There are a lot more interesting people here than I ever had in any of my classes, so the change is nice. Even met a few humans I can talk to."

Maz looked down. Her handheld blinked insistently from its spot on her lap as the timer she'd set at the beginning of the call counted down to phase two.

"Do you think you're going to get any action? Your ship, I mean. I've been worried." Maz watched Nines' expression shift from jovial to concentrated. She hoped the change wasn't too obvious.

"What, in a state-of-the-art Grzzh dreadnaught like the *Protectorate Maul*? Oh, *no*, I doubt we're going to do any fighting any time soon. We're probably just gonna waste these top-notch stealth and weapons systems wandering through the Dyson Field with the rest of the fleet, and scoop up any rebel patrols we find. We're thinking we'll just do passive defensive patterns for the next few cycles."

"Yeah, it's not like the sensors back on the station detected a jump pattern straight from the *Maul*'s patrol route into the heart of the rebel base, like we even know where that is. You're *totally* better off sticking with the fleet and patrolling."

"Oh, really? No point in spending time searching for those routes, then. Man, I guess the navy won't get any chances to catch the rebels with their pants down. *What a bummer,*" Nines said. Maz tried not to wince at her girlfriend's over-inflection.

"Hope you don't die of boredom, babe," Maz said, smiling.

Nines laughed. "Oh, I hope I don't die at all! That'd be nice." She smiled and reached her hand out to brush the screen with her fingertips. "Miss you, darlin'."

"I miss you, too. Feels like you've been gone forever."

"You're telling me. It's still so weird to be off the station." Nines looked over her shoulder to something off-screen and turned back to Maz. "I think I need to get going, Maz. Looks like Burg needs me to fill out some forms."

"I should start getting ready, too. Love you, Nines."

"Love you, too, Maz. Have fun tonight!"

"Here's hoping. You, too."

"Oh, I know I will."

Maz tapped hesitantly at her handheld and Nines disappeared from the cabin window, leaving only the debris-shrouded stars of the Dyson Field to mark her passage.

"Sarcasm? Your groundbreaking new military code is sarcasm?" A young man in a blue Consortium military jacket hoisted himself upward from his relaxed lean against Maz's apartment wall. Like most of Maz's interactions with Security Captain Simon DuGalle, the officer took painstaking effort to appear as nonchalant as possible—a typical social paradox undertaken by someone who wanted to impress a member of the interested sex without their conscious acknowledgement. Unfortunately for DuGalle, Maz had some experience in that regard.

"It'll be obsolete as soon as the war's over, I think. If we're unlucky, it'll be a bit sooner," Maz said, rising from her chair and slipping her handheld into her pocket, "But, yes, my code is sarcasm. There are a few Consortium species incapable of prosodic speech, but most of them get used to interpreting it after a few years in the galactic community. Same with the Grrzh: Rather than communicating intent with tonally implicit content, they use explicit language to communicate emotional meaning.

"So even if the Grrzh rebels can crack the navy's encryption, which they've proven capable of doing because they essentially share the same coding methods, then manage to translate Anthrop, which the rebels have never heard before but can manage with some decent software, they still won't have a method for discerning which parts of the communication are genuine."

DuGalle blinked, inhaled, opened his mouth, and closed it again. "I think I understood about a third of those words," he admitted after a moment.

"You took twice as many Consortium cross-culture lectures than I did! You're the head of security for one of the most integrated stations in Consortium space!" Maz said. She watched in amusement as DuGalle winced sheepish, and smiled. She was about as romantically interested in him as she would be a toothbrush, but she could not deny that the captain was an outwardly charming man.

"The Grrzh produce a sort of humming buzz to communicate, right? They use varying pitch and intervals to produce words?" Maz asked. As she spoke, she walked to her apartment's book-strewn dinner table and plucked a dress coat from the back of one of its chairs.

"Right," DuGalle said.

"Well, the way that their language evolved, their speech doesn't use differing vocal tones to communicate additional meanings, like emotion. They just use their words to do it for them instead." Maz shrugged the coat on, checked the pocket for her Consortium consultant badge, and slipped her handheld in alongside it.

"So when you talk sarcastically, they can't understand you?"

"Sort of. Their speech might as well be written text, so when they hear sarcasm they aren't even aware that there's a hidden meaning to understand. So far, they've taken every message they've intercepted literally, and the *Protectorate Maul* has been able to catch them completely unaware on several occasions. We've even experimented with allowing the rebels to intercept us so we could bait them and the outcome has been favorable. Plus, according to a few interceptions of our own, it's pissing the rebels off to no end," Maz said. She tried and failed not to seem overeager—she hadn't had a chance to discuss the intricacies of her project with anyone but Nines, and was glad for the chance to talk about her work. DuGalle nodded in apparent understanding.

"The beauty of it is that the only reason it works on the Grzzh rebels is that they're fanatically against integrating with the Consortium, and we're the only ones who could possibly explain to them how it works. Racism is literally losing a war for them."

"So you say," DuGalle said. There was something about the way his mouth was set that told Maz she was irritating the officer. He was a military man, after all, and she was treading in his territory without subjecting herself to the endemic risk—or maybe he was jealous that the embassy had found a simple way to help the Grzzh that didn't involve building them a warship.

"Well, we'll see," Maz said. "The *Protectorate Maul*'s probably just scanned for the jump point we found. They'll pop into the rebel base of operations while we're out tonight. I'm willing to bet it's unguarded while the rebels search for patrols, and the base will be dispatched by the time we get back. The embassy thinks there's a chance that it'll win us the war."

"Wait, we've won already?" DuGalle asked.

"Like I said, I'm willing to wager. Why else would I take tonight off to get everyone together and celebrate?"

DuGalle keyed the pad for Maz's front door and wordlessly followed her into the apartment hallway. The officer plainly had something to say, but he was holding back.

"What's wrong, Simon?" Maz asked eventually.

"You just sent a loved one into a combat zone and you want to make bets?" His posture was stiff, his back and shoulders rigid as they walked.

"I meant that colloquially, but you know what? Sure. I'll bet with you. I'll bet that my months of research, my considerable efforts and sacrifice to get this program moving, and my very capable girlfriend have better odds than your uninformed skepticism." Maz stopped walking, and DuGalle halted beside her. His face twitched with indignant guilt, and Maz smiled and reached for his hand. "I understand your doubts, but we've put more thought into this than you appreciate. Okay? Let's have an enjoyable evening. We can get back to the military talk tomorrow."

DuGalle sighed. "All right. I'm sorry. But this is playing with fire, Maz. I wouldn't want to be in your shoes when it doesn't work."

"You know, that's what my mom said about Nines and I when we started dating. Your concern is noted, big guy. But trust me—it'll work."

Grrzh Dreadnought Protectorate Maul, *Outside Former Grrzh Rebel Base*

"Dang, I can't believe that worked as well as it did!" Nines said, as she swung her maintenance tug into one of the *Protectorate Maul*'s cavernous docking bays, an incapacitated rebel lifeboat gripped in her ship's manipulator arms. The diminutive craft puttered to the refueling station the warship's crew had converted for her, where it lowered the captive lifeboat to the hangar deck before dropping it the remaining two meters into the center of a waiting squad of Grrzh marines. Just beyond the translucent docking bay shield, the gargantuan metal shards of the Dyson Field slowly spun in the disturbance caused by the detonating rebel base of operations.

"Satisfied. It did seem to go well. Thank you for helping our crews with salvage and rescue," Burg said through the tug's comms.

"Eh, it's the least I can do," Nines said as she keyed in the tug's docking sequence. Around her little ship, squadrons of one-man Grrzh craft landed and departed as automated refit drones swapped their combat kits for more appropriate cleanup apparatuses. One drone regarded Nines's ship momentarily before it puttered away, unable to decipher the ship's foreign construction.

Nines stepped out of the roaring hangar and into the shimmering olive green access hallway, where Burg waited. The hunched Grrzh diplomat tapped the fingers of her secondary arm-cluster together, while the primary cluster swept outward in a traditional Grrzh greeting, rotating her delicate wrists and fanning her fingers. Nines would have attempted returning the gesture, but Burg had informed her that her first few trials were almost offensively bad. Nines simply settled for a friendly wave before leaning one shoulder against the wall.

"What's up? Why'd you call me in?" she asked. Her small glass handheld vibrated on her belt as the wing-like fixtures in Burg's face began to oscillate, beating together to create the deep hum of Grrzh speech.

"Unsure," the handheld interpreted, translating Burgh's buzzing into an amiable but monotone female voice. "The bridge officers requested an opportunity to speak with you."

"Uh-oh. Am I going alone?"

"Reassuring. No I shall accompany you. They might mean well but they are intimidating and I do not think that their capacity to understand your speech has improved since the last time you spoke to them. Helpful. If it is required I can translate for your benefit," Burg said, the arch of her chitinous bulk lowering slightly. Nines suspected that Burg's posture was a Grrzh sign of trust or comfort, but she wasn't entirely sure—body language was more Maz's cup of tea.

"Aw, thanks, Burg. That bridge gives me the creeps," Nines said.

"Warm. It is my pleasure." The two walked to a door for one of the ship trams, where Burg keyed in a transport request. As they waited, Burg's second forearm cluster entwined its fingers together, one hand picking at the gaps in the chitin that separated her knuckles.

"Inquisitive," the Grrzh hummed, "Where will you go now that the war is over."

Nines blinked in surprise. "You know, I hadn't thought that far ahead. I wasn't really planning long-term as far as this program was concerned. I figure I'll probably head back home to the station. Get a bowl from my favorite noodle joint, hug Maz so hard we both pass out, beg for my old job at Hull Maintenance. That kinda stuff."

"Curious. You miss home." The elevator arrived and both stepped in. Nines watched Burg tap in the bridge access code and tried her best not to memorize it for later, but failed. Old habits died hard.

"Well, yeah! Is that weird?" Nines asked.

"Expository. No I was simply confused by the degree

of excitement you displayed when you first began this assignment and the excitement you display now as you are about to end it."

"What, the Grrzh don't get homesick?"

"Expository. Not particularly we do not place emphasis on home or family and instead emphasize the individual. Ruminating. I believe it may have something to do with our insecurity about evolving from insectoid races in a galaxy dominated by primate and reptilian types, but I am no historian."

Nines smiled and propped herself against the elevator wall. "Man, I can't imagine that. I grew up on the station, you know? The administrators named me after the bulkhead they found me in. Part of that was why I took the job, though. Maz has been everywhere and she has all these stories. I kinda wanted one of those stories for myself, but now I've got it, I'd like to hop back in my big metal bubble. It's got all my favorite creature comforts and all the folks I love."

There was a pause, even after her handheld finished translating Nines' speech into Grrzh. After a few uncomfortable seconds, Burg spoke again. "Inquiring. Is the Consortium station truly the only place with people you care for."

Nines cocked her head. "What do you—" she began, before the elevator halted and the doors slid open. Nines winced as she stared into the imposing darkness of the *Protectorate Maul*'s unlit bridge. While Consortium and Grrzh engineers had collaborated together to build most of the dreadnaught, the bridge and the majority of the living quarters were solely Grrzh design.

Burg had explained once that the Grrzh military saw light as a distraction, and that even since their homeworld-bound days had kept strategic tents dark to prevent the intrusion of visual stimuli. This meant that even though every member of the bridge crew was plugged into the ship's systems via virtual reality masks,

the bridge was still almost entirely unlit but for a few
digital consoles and the light from Nines' elevator.

It also meant that Nines was expected to stand in
the center of a dark, three-tiered room surrounded by
a legion of masked bug-people. Her time on the station
had pushed her far from anthropocentrism, but the sight
still unsettled her. She jumped when she felt a hand on
her shoulder, but when she realized it was Burg trying
to comfort her she smiled back and patted her friend's
fingers.

"Formalpleasestepintothechamberandallowthe
elevatordoorstoclose," Nines' handheld dirged.

"Oh! Sorry," Nines said, and took a quick step inside
the chamber. As soon as Burg stepped in behind her, the
door slid shut with a sound like a sheathing sword and
immersed the two in darkness.

Nines tried to find which of the Grrzh her handheld
was translating, but behind their interface masks none of
the bridge crew seemed to be looking in her direction.

"Gratefulyourassistanceisgreatlyappreciatedwithout
youthisdecisivevictorywouldnothavebeenpossible."

"Yes, of course—" Nines continued to search the
crowd for a sir or madam to address, but still found none.
"—Your...Honor. It has been my pleasure to assist, and
to grow more familiar with your culture. Ambassadress
Burg has been a great help in this regard."

"Warmitisgoodtohearthatwecouldbringourcultures
closertogetherindeedevenastheremainderoftherebelfleet
fliesstraightintothejawsofyourConsortiumwarbaseour
bondsgrowcloserinheartsandinblood."

"I'm pleased to hear that we can continue to grow
closer as a community—" Nines was cut off as Burg tightened her grip on her shoulder. Nines turned back and
met Burg's eyes, and the Grrzh shook her head frantically.
"What? Did I miss something?" Nines asked.

"Alarmed. They have just informed you that the
rebels have plotted a course toward your Consortium

space station."

"They're *what*?" Nines shouted.

"Confusedisthisnotatacticalroutetheywillsurelybe
crushedbyyoursuperiordefenses."

"No, the station isn't a military installation! It's
almost entirely a civilian population; a refit and refuel
station at best! The security ships won't be able to fend off
an entire fleet!"

There was a pause.

"SuspiciousisthismoreofyourtonalduplicityIcannot
tell."

"Tonal duplicity? You mean sarcasm?" Nines asked.

"NervousItakethatasano."

Dyson Field Station Embassy

Maz and Simon stumbled through the Consortium
embassy doors, leaning on one another for support.

"Oh my God, I've never seen someone dance that
badly before," Maz said, flattening the collar of her jacket.

"I wasn't that bad!" DuGalle said.

"You made that Iliff girl cry!"

"She shouldn't watch bar dance floors if she can't
take a little human mambo!"

"She was so innocent! So young! And you come
along, rolling around like a creature made entirely out of
shoulders and you expose her to a new world of darkness
and uncertainty!"

"I don't—whoa. This isn't your apartment," DuGalle
said, looking up at the embassy ceiling's wide blue arch-
ways. When the sprawling architecture began to unravel
like a throbbing cobalt fractal, he wished he had not.

"Sounds like a certain shoulder golem's optimistic
about his chances. Why don't you—" Maz blinked as she
saw the empty digital terminals and processing equipment. "Oh, wow. It really isn't. I must have punched in my

elevator code for work instead of going home."

"I told you that you needed a night out! You're a work-aholic!" DuGalle said, wedging his back against a desk. Something chirped in his breast pocket, and he swatted at his chest in an attempt to quiet it.

"I can't be a workaholic if I'm drunk! That's *ex post facto* on 'holism, I think..." Maz trailed off. A row away from her, a terminal had flickered to life. She moved closer and keyed up a pending alert. Security drones detected an intrusion signal lurking beyond the Dyson field. "Hey, DuGalle, did you—"

She turned to face DuGalle, who had finally managed to retrieve his chirping handheld from his breast pocket and answer it. To Maz's horror, the security captain went white as a sheet.

"Grrzh rebel ships are waiting outside the Dyson field. Security ships are asking me what to do. Oh gods..."

Maz dug her wallet out of her jacket pockets and plucked two pills from a capsule in one of its compart-ments. She swallowed one and handed the second to DuGalle, who refused it and tapped an implant nodule behind his left ear. Maz counted to six and felt the effects of the alcohol wash away as her organs kicked into overdrive to metabolize it.

"They're hailing us," Maz said, tapping the blinking terminal. "We won't be able to get a senior ambassador here for another fifteen minutes."

"Stall them. I need to coordinate with the security attaché," DuGalle said. Maz nodded and opened the fre-quency between the embassy and the Grrzh ship. A large Grrzh seated in a massive captain's chair gesticulated wildly with both its arm-clusters.

"FuriousConsortiummixedracescumstandand deliver," the terminal translated in dull monotone. Maz recognized the figure onscreen as the Grrzh rebels' ruthless Admiral Ferrnj.

Over Maz's shoulder, DuGalle muttered to himself

as he tapped at his handheld's screen. "Why the hell are they here? We haven't been a strategically significant target since the beginning of the war! They're so far past their front line they might as well be—"

"Righteousyourdeceitfuloppositespeechhascostus everything.Demandingwhereisthefleshycharlatancalled Maz."

"Oh. Uh-oh," Maz said.

"For a civilization that doesn't understand sarcasm, they're just as irritated by it as anyone else," DuGalle said over her shoulder. Maz toggled the transmit setting.

"This is Maz, Dyson Station Embassy Journeyman Behaviorist. Why have you come to our station?" The Grrzh captain straightened visibly in his seat.

"Defiantwehavecometodiehonorablyonthespears ofthetruevictorsinthiswar.Bitterourownkindcouldonly defeatuswiththeaidofyourtechnologyandmanipulation."

"They what?" Maz said to herself. A second Grrzh ducked into frame.

"Plaintiveapologiessirbutthereareonlyahandfulof Consortiumfrigatespresent.Regretfulwewillnotbeable toperishinbattleagainstafleetthisfeeble." Admiral Ferrnj turned to his subordinate, his antennae lowered in surprise.

"Astonished," he said, slower than Maz had heard any Grrzh speak. "Ohmygoodness."

Grrzh Dreadnaught Protectorate Maul, *Dyson Field*

Nines tapped furiously at her cabin terminal, cycling through the ship's communication arrays.

"Concerned. Is there anything I can do," Burg asked behind her.

"Nope," Nines said. She didn't know too much about hyperluminal communication, but she didn't think that there was any method available to the *Protectorate Maul* that could contact a far-off Consortium fleet without also letting the rebel fleet know they were coming. There were plenty of ways to mask a short-range transmission, but contacting anyone outside the Dyson Field was another matter entirely.

"Nervous. We have arrived at the station but four out of five of the security fleet have been damaged beyond combat capabilities all have retreated into the cover of the Dyson Field the remaining rebel ships have formed a holding pattern around the station." Burg tapped at her own handheld, a gift Nines had provided the ambassadress at the start of her journey.

"A holding pattern?" Nines asked.

"Apprehensive. Yes they seem to want to take the station or the personnel inside it hostage."

Nines rubbed at her temples. "Can you send a field projection to my terminal?"

"Helpful. I assume that you are requesting my compliance rather than assessing my ability to—"

"Please, Burg. Now."

"Concerned. You are upset." Burg's arm clusters fidgeted.

"Yes, Burg! I'm terrified! My home and my girlfriend are in mortal danger and I can't do anything about it! Please, just send the projection!"

Burg tapped silently at her handheld and Nines' terminal received a three-dimensional diagram of the rebel fleet's positions. The security fleet, although hopelessly outmanned, still outgunned the rebel fleet and had inflicted significant losses. The five ellipsoid ships huddled behind the shattered metal of the Dyson field, cut off from the seven remaining knife-shaped Grrzh battlecruisers. The largest had connected itself to the Consortium station using what looked to Nines like a primitive boarding umbilical.

"It seems like their capital ship's docked with the station," Nines said.

"Informative. A last-ditch rebel tactic if any ships try to interfere while their shock troops storm the station they detonate the ship's engines and claim as many civilian lives as possible," Burg said. Nines said nothing as she rotated the image, trying to find something she hadn't seen yet.

"Then we can't discharge our weapons. All we can do is move and talk. What the hell can we—" Nines froze. "We get in close! We use the *Maul*'s stealth systems to get in there before they see us coming and shield the station from the blast!"

"Concerned. That does not sound like a safe plan we should wait for Consortium forces."

"Wait? We can't wait, we don't even know if help is coming! Look, even with just civilian grade armor and shielding, the detonation would only make a divot in the station's surface. Problem is, a divot in a station that size could still cost hundreds of civilian lives, if not thousands. But put some distance and a nearly indestructible military dreadnought between the station and the explosion—"

"Frustrated. Why are you so desperate to risk our lives."

"I'm desperate because everything I know and love is on that station! I can't stand by and do nothing while a racist militant psychopath runs rampant in my home!" Nines shouted. She tried to remember the tricks Maz had taught her to calm herself down, but fear and fury coursed through her skull.

"Helpful. Perhaps there is a new home for you here instead and maybe a new love," Burg said. Nines's breath caught in her throat. Burg stooped over, both arm clusters picking erratically at her chitinous fingers.

"Is that what this is about? Are you trying to talk me out of this just so...so you can get in my pants?" Nines asked.

"Distressed. I am not familiar with this euphemism

perhaps if we could—"

"No. No, I'm done. If you're not going to help me, I'm going to the bridge," Nines said, struggling to keep her voice level. She stood and pushed her way past Burg, storming out the door toward the ship trams. The dormitory hallways, normally bustling with Grrzh, had been emptied of all family and personnel as they rushed for bunkers and action stations. Regardless, Nines did her best to keep her composure as she called for a tram. The door slid soundlessly open and she stepped inside.

Nines took a deep breath and entered Burg's administrative code for the *Protectorate Maul*'s bridge. The terminal shrieked an error message back at her. She growled and entered the code again. Another error. She had to be off by only one digit; she had never forgotten a code before. Another entry, another shriek, and a toneless Grrzh voice notifying her that another erroneous entry would result in a lockout.

Nines roared and sunk to her knees, slamming her fist against the tram wall. A familiar feeling of helplessness crept over her, spreading through her limbs and seeping into her core in a way she hadn't felt since she was a child, orphaned in a claustrophobic world of bulkheads and cold vacuum.

She was barely aware of fingers tapping at the terminal above her, and the tram doors sliding shut behind her like a sheathing sword. Nines felt the reassuring grip of a Grrzh hand press down on her shoulder, and she looked up to see Burg.

"Morose. I understand if you do not care for me but I want you to be happy I should not have allowed my feelings to interfere at such an inappropriate time and I apologi—" Nines cut the ambassadress off by throwing her arms around the Grrzh's waist.

"Thank you," she said.

"You are welcome. Now let us save your home."

Dyson Field Station Embassy

"TriumphantthisisAdmiralFerrnjwehavecaptured yourfeebleConsortiumembassy," Admiral Ferrnj said into the embassy terminal, his fingers wrapped around Maz's skull. "Witnessthemightofaunifiedraceandtremble."

Maz did her best not to roll her eyes. Despite his progress, the Grrzh was out of his depth. He had avoided all of the station's strategic points—armories, defense systems, and life support—to follow Maz's signal straight to the embassy. There, he had lost a large chunk of his boarding party trying to fight past Captain DuGalle, who had turned their insides to steaming slurry with a military-grade microwave projector the size of a walnut. DuGalle lay unconscious but alive on the other side of the room, his personal shield having dampened a blow which Ferrnj assumed lethal.

"DeterminedIwilldestroythisstationandtakethis meatyfalsifierfortorture."

"Could you please stop talking about my meat? I understand the biological gap, but it's still pretty unsettling," Maz said. She felt the massive Grrzh apply pressure to her skull and gasped in pain.

"Hey! Hands off my lady, asshat!" Nines' voice called from the embassy terminal.

"Nines! Where are you?"

"Oh, nowhere near close enough to see the predicament you're in," Nines said. Maz tried to find her girlfriend in the terminal display, but shadow obscured the onscreen image.

"Indignantyoursquishydeceivingpartnerhasarrived toolate." The admiral paused.

"Confuseddoesthatmeanthatsheiscloseorthatsheisfar away."

"Right, like I'd tell you that," Maz said.

"Requestingyeswouldyouplease."

"Anyway," Nines interjected, "There wasn't any *possible* way that we could figure out how to get close to you, especially in a sneaky-ass dreadnaught like this. So there was no hope of me convincing the bridge's crew to do something outrageously stupid like coming to save you. And there certainly won't be anyone for the remaining Consortium ships to provide covering fire for in a last-ditch attempt to save the station."

"Confidentnowthereisnowaythatisafarce."

Dyson Field

The *Protectorate Maul* emerged from behind the cover of the Dyson Field and launched itself toward the Consortium space station, leaving only a cosmic whisper of a heat signature in its wake. The dreadnaught continued to pick up speed as the last security frigate slid into view from beyond the Dyson Field. The remaining Grrzh warships saw the *Maul* too late, and the ship's traditional knifelike design drove a wedge between the docked rebel capital ship and the space station.

The side of the *Maul*'s prow bounced off the station's hull, their kinetic fields repulsing the dreadnaught's impact, but the rebel battlecruiser was not as fortunate. The docking umbilical snapped like a dry reed as the dreadnaught plowed through the gap between the two structures. The battlecruiser's hull, already slightly damaged from the earlier battle, buckled under the impact and the ship hurtled helplessly into space. Inside, the rebel crew tried to reverse the ship's detonation sequence as they scrambled to grasp what was happening, but automated systems under the admiral's command initiated the countdown regardless.

The battlecruiser drifted almost half a kilometer away from the station before the chain reaction in its engines consumed it from the inside out. Heat washed over the *Protectorate Maul*, but the dreadnaught's shields held. Weapons discharge from the *Maul* and the Consortium frigate in the Dyson Field caught the remaining rebel warships in an unforgiving pincer of fire. In moments, only dust and angry echoes remained of the Grrzh rebel fleet.

Protectorate Maul, *Outside Dyson Field Station*

Nines cheered from the bridge of the *Protectorate Maul* and turned to hug Burg once more. She raised her handheld again to find Admiral Ferrnj and his remaining rebel troops staring slackly at the projection she had conjured of the carnage.

"Lay down your arms, Admiral Ferrnj," Nines said. "Consortium security will pick you up shortly, and they'll be happy to avoid any more bloodshed."

The boarders with Ferrnj dropped their weapons without complaint, but the rebel admiral did not move.

"Don't do anything you'll regret, Admiral," Nines heard Maz say. The Grrzh looked to his subordinates and his posture began to droop, his arm clusters loosening their grip on his massive ballistic rifle. Something off-screen caught his eye, and his back straightened.

"AngryIwillnotsurrendertoagalaxyofmanipulatorsI willfindnorestinyourprisons," the Grrzh said, tightening his grip on Maz and forcing her to follow him out of the terminal's line of sight.

"Maz? Maz!" Nines shouted into her handheld. The embassy doors opened and the last of the Grrzh troops submitted to the Consortium security team that stormed in, but formed a semicircle around the door to block further access to the room.

"He's taking her! Stop him! Please!" Nines shouted into her handheld. If the security team heard her, they gave no sign. Nines lowered her handheld and cut the connection. She turned to the bridge officers.

"I think Ferrnj found the embassy lifeboats. He'll probably force Maz to give him the code out, but your fighters can catch him as he emerges." She approached a viewscreen of the station's exterior and tried to recall what she remembered from her days in hull repair. "The embassy's lifeboat channel should lead to...this exit here. It'll come out here; I'm sure of it," she said, pointing to a cluster of hatches in the station's side. She looked back to the Grrzh officers, who remained motionless.

"Well?" she asked.

"Hesitantwehaveriskedonediplomaticincident already," one of them said.

"Wedonotwanttoriskasecondbyinadvertentlykillinga Consortiumambassadress."

"She'll die either way if you just sit here!" Nines said. "All right, you know what? Sure. I'll leave her to die. Sounds like an awesome idea. I'm gonna go back to my cabin and twiddle my thumbs." Nines turned and stepped into the bridge tram, Burg following close behind. The doors shut behind them both, and the bridge was dark and silent once more. One officer raised his virtual mask to look at the rest.

"Hopefuldoyouthinkshemeantit?"

Emergency Lifeboat, Eighty Meters From Consortium Station and Counting

Maz closed her eyes to stop her vision from swimming. Ferrnj had slammed her head against the lifeboat door when she had refused to give him access, and the haze refused to clear. The Grrzh held his rifle barrel pointed at her temple, but his eyes were fixed straight ahead as he piloted the lifeboat in a beeline for the Dyson Field.

"Maz, you out there?" Nines voice asked over the

lifeboat radio. Admiral Ferrnj glanced at Maz before fixing his gaze back on the pilot's screen.

"SeethingtellherthatIwillkillyouifshedoesnotbackoff."

"You hear that, Nines?" Maz asked.

"Sure did," Nines said. "I assume he's got you dead to rights in there, huh? No way to escape, even with a bit of help?"

Maz looked to the Grrzh next to her, who did not meet her gaze. She glanced at the console between them, where a medical kit and a compact rad-projector rested under a layer of emergency webbing.

"No, nothing to be done," Maz said. "Whatever you try, there's no way it's going to work."

Nines' Maintenance Tug, Twenty Meters From Emergency Lifeboat and Closing

"Never heard *that* one before," Nines said, opening the throttle.

THROUGH THE NEVER

Eneasz Brodski

The human pilot smashed a bottle of their intoxicant into the transport's virgin hull, the impact blossoming into a tiny nova of glass and golden liquid. Zierr swished her tails politely, cheering with everyone else out of obligation. There was no good reason for her not to attend this ceremony. It wasn't the strangest custom, and she kept telling herself that every culture had their eccentricities. But the humans' rituals were always so damned public. Zierr didn't like public. She kept to herself.

Munith shimmied to her side. "Once you're en route, this will all have been worth it," Munith whispered through an antenna, uninvited. She resisted the impulse to slap his antenna away. It wasn't uncommon for exes to retain that familiarity, even if it had been years. His presumptuousness was almost comforting. That cockiness had drawn her once. To be honest, it still worked well for him.

"Social bonding is very important to humans," he continued, "Go up and exchange touches at some point. It makes you more real to him."

"Ugh, no," Zierr replied. "They're too wriggly. Did you have to touch it much?"

"Eh...'have to' is relative. The project didn't demand much, no." Munith had designed the human interface for this new transport. "But there was plenty of touching that 'had to' be done to keep them comfortable. A touch at every greeting and leave-taking, and often other incidentals. You get used to it."

Zierr squirmed with discomfort. "You should spend more time with your own kind—I think they're rubbing off on you."

Munith's antenna trembled in amusement. "Not possible. They have the most shattered minds of any species, they couldn't rub off on another species even if we wanted it. We think that's why they're so resilient, and why they constantly latch on to others."

Of course by "we" he meant the broader human-research community, rather than Zierr and the rest of the gathered transport design team. He delighted in learning everything he could about these squirmy little creatures with the steel psyches. It reminded her of their time together, and brought with it an unwelcome melancholy ache. Fortunately, he'd spent most of his time at this project with the volunteer human and Zierr hadn't run into him often.

"This sort of public bonding is a weak form of human soul-joining, across many minds at once. Come on." Munith took a shuffling quarter-stride toward the human.

Zierr recoiled. "Oh my god, they soul-join across species?"

"Oh, lay off, it barely even counts. It's the lightest psychic touch. They have to mediate it across air vibrations and physical contact. Aren't you the least bit interested in what makes them so hard to crack?"

"No. I'm not crazy." But she relented and followed him. The discovery of the human race had revolutionized warp transportation. It couldn't hurt to be in their pilot's good graces.

Zierr did her best not to think about what this was like for the human as she fondled his little hand in an up-and-down pumping motion, and let him pat her shoulder mounds. He bared his teeth from within the furry bush that covered most of his face—their way of smiling. She really hoped this was worth it.

Zierr's mother had worked in pilot recovery, pre-humanity. Not on the front lines, which was mostly corpse-recovery. Zierr's mother worked in rehabilitation. She saw the few who had been successfully apprehended *before* they could force open the airlocks, or override the safeties in the medbay. She was given the survivors. The ones that clutched their antenna against their bodies, staring voiceless into dimensions beyond physical sight. The ones that breathed an endless stream of words, each one intelligible, and consistent with the words before and after it, but in aggregate the words wove together into a single endless sentence without any meaning...*worm summoning the twisting world with the power of their lives while who we are cannot be asked for the reason that never pursues...*

"We can't just write them off," Zierr's mother said. "They've given their lives to keep our species relevant. We owe them."

When she was older, Zierr sought out her mother's former mates. Most wouldn't talk about her. They folded their antenna and pulled away. Only Jathem took her into his confidence, let her taste his over-sweet regrets.

"Yeah, she would tell me the same things," he confirmed. "Species self-determination and all that. It makes a great slogan, doesn't it?" He sighed, a light taste. "And of course we can't cede the galaxy to the other races. But people like your mother, people who work in recovery... well, that's not the real reason they do it. If you hear their private words, you can taste the truth. She had to save everyone. Save the world, the species, maybe the galaxy. It's a noble sort of broken, but it's still broken."

Zierr should have done more. Her father had died before her birth, but she could have told her teachers.

She'd known something was wrong, even at her age. Her mother's words had listed toward salt for months. Near the end, no utterance was free of saline undertones. Even discussing Zierr's schoolwork came with a taste of briny dread; an ever-present seasoning of despair.

"People like your mother feel too much of others' emotions," Jathem said, "even without tasting them. They mean well, but they can't let go. Your mother was doomed from the start. She should have never stepped within a mile of a pilot."

Jathem had left before the end. Maybe he'd felt it coming.

"Why wasn't I enough?" Munith asked her, a few weeks after the design team had been assembled. They'd stayed late after a team dinner, once the others had left, catching up over a slow hookah. He had aged gracefully. The short furs of his muzzle and crest were touched with symmetrical silver streaks—just enough to make him look distinguished.

Zierr sighed, wondering if she should answer. Would it make the workplace more uncomfortable to leave this hanging, or to let him know? She didn't think he'd be satisfied with her answer anyway.

"How many other mates did you have while we were together?" she asked him in reply.

"None." Answered without hesitation.

"And how many did I have?"

"Um...just Cerric I think? Wait, Dnyira, too, for a few months."

"Well, there you go."

Munith's antenna soured slightly. "I wasn't popular enough for you?" He studied her face. "You know how busy I was. Hell, I still am. These humans are fascinating! They shouldn't be able to function, but here they are, not just walking but creating...well, never mind. The point is, I don't have time for a lot of relationships. So what? You weren't the sort of person to care about popularity."

Zierr shifted to her other elbow and pulled from the hookah. She took a moment before answering: "I don't have a lot of time either, Munith"—she exhaled—"but I didn't make that your problem. You think warp engineering leaves me with a lot of spare hours? I *made* time for what was important. You could have, too."

"I didn't want any other mates."

And there it was. That selfishness again, the counterpart to his cockiness. She let him taste her growing frustration.

"Right. You laid all your emotions and needs on me, instead of spreading them out. I never did that to you. You saved time by overloading me. Don't you get how intolerable that is?" Even for someone as attractive as Munith.

"You didn't have to though! Didn't you read any of the mono-amory books I lent you? You could have put everything on me as well, and we'd be equal. It's so simple. Just, why...why wasn't I enough?"

Oh god. Zierr pulled her antenna away. He didn't get it. He would never get it.

"People die, you know," she told him simply, via sound. "Or they change. Or they leave. Who did you have to fall back on when I left?"

"I had my parents. And my friends."

"No mates. It hurt to leave you. You know that?" Zierr reached out again, let him taste the remnants of that panic. The knowledge that she was leaving him with no one. "But you weren't trying to find anyone else. I can't be your savior. I can't be your world. It's too damn much to heap on one person. What did you tell me on our anniversary?"

"I want you to be my everything," they both said in unison. Him with hope, her with anger.

"Never," she continued, reaching for her com. "I will never be anyone's everything. Everything is too much. You can't expect that from me."

"I should have lied to you?"

"You should have someone else to rely on if I die. Died. You know what, I'm not having this conversation again. I'm sorry I'm not comfortable with your weird social movement. Let's call it a night." Zierr pulled out her com-pad, checked her portion of the bill, and approved a payment transfer.

"Of course." Munith reached for his com as well. "Sorry. I know it's not for everyone. I won't bring it up again. Do you wanna split a ride back?"

Zierr hesitated. She didn't remotely want that, but it could head off awkwardness over the coming months to bury their differences.

"All right." She stood, mentally reaching for any other subject. "Hey, did you hear they've chosen our human? We might meet it as soon as next month."

"Him," Munith corrected, following her lead. "They dislike 'it.' Enough so that they prefer using the term 'they' as a singular if you don't know their gender."

"Huh, that's bizarre."

"That's not even the half of it..."

It wasn't until a full year after the burial that Zierr summoned up the courage to open her mother's journal. She started at the end.

It's a single, endless scream. It doesn't ever stop.

Haven't slept in days. The more I try to forget, the harder it gets. Should have retired years ago. Moved on. Or just not thought about it.

NEVER THINK ABOUT IT

Now it's just me and God. All those little pieces. One tiny shard from each pilot. Who knew? How could I have known? Why would there be any pattern?

Can't stop. See the pattern everywhere. They knew. Every word meant stay away. Stay away. Don't see. Don't think.

Oh God. All those little shards. I collected them. Stuck them all in my brain. Then jumble and shake and stab, stab, stab. Look there! Is that a picture? Is that a pattern? Look harder...

Don't look. Never look. All the pieces come together in a mosaic. It's not madness. Not rambling. It's a warning. Who are you?

I can't ever tell anyone. I am infected. If anyone else knows, they will be too. It grows in your mind. How to tell if someone can take this curse? Been waiting too long. If I tell anyone, they might tell another. Someone less equipped to handle it. It'll spread and spread and spread until there is nothing left. No, not an option.

We are all dust. We return. It is not our place to challenge.

No one else knows. That's the only saving grace. I can't end that. Can't end it all. This stays inside me, and me alone.

Have to stop thinking about this. There must be a way.

That final entry had been dated nearly eight months before The Day. The day Zierr had come home from school to find her mother in a cold bath tub. The bright pink water looked like what rose tears would look like, if roses had eyes for crying. At first she had thought it was some sort of fancy perfume. But no perfume would smell like that.

She didn't bother reading any other entries.

Two days after the human's christening ceremony, the day before the new transport's maiden voyage, Zierr wandered the quiet ship. She stopped in the observatory, taking in the great glass dome above. Beyond it, only the roof of the massive construction hanger.

"Ever seen a warp rift?" asked a squeaky voice. Zierr turned to regard the human, ambling up to her on his two unlikely legs.

"Yes."

"Ah, one of the lucky few." The warp was a purely psychic phenomenon, and so couldn't be recorded or amplified by physical instruments. The only way to "see" warp space was to get close to a warp rift in person. "They say no one ever forgets their first time. I was twelve years old when I saw mine. We were on humanity's very first colony ship. Pioneers. Runs in the family."

"I was young, too. My mother worked in interstellar transportation. She thought it was important I see what made galactic civilization possible."

Warp space couldn't be properly conveyed by any means. One had to see it for oneself. That didn't stop artists and directors from trying, of course. Visual portrayals showed slowly swirling blues and whites, underlit with flashes of many-hued lightnings. Musical accompaniment began gentle and wondrous, swelling slowly to stirring peaks, and was always subtly hypnotic. Tastes invariably consisted of awe and peace.

In Zierr's opinion, all such attempts were failures. Nothing compared to being near a rift. To see a rift was to gaze upon the face of God.

The human looked up through the observation dome, his eyes distant, as if he could see past the hanger roof, past the atmosphere and the days of travel in space. As if warp space was just above him, and he could reach out and touch it if he chose. "When I saw it," he said, "I knew at once that if I ever cried again, I would be crying for the perfection of the warp. It was so beautiful it hurt. There was nothing else in all creation."

Zierr looked up at the hanger roof. There was nothing there but steel beams and iron sheeting.

"My mother lost her last mate not long before our trip to see it," Zierr volunteered. Munith said humans liked this sort of thing. "She'd been shedding them for a while. Now, I think it was on purpose, but at the time all I knew was that my world was being stripped away one person at a time. I was too young for mates of my own, so it was just her and me, crammed in this tiny shuttle with a dozen strangers. Religious fanatics, most of them. All of us were alone, especially when we were all together. It was awful.

"Then on the fifth day we reach the warp rift, and it just sort of blooms across your entire being, you know?" The human nodded—an agreement. "And suddenly, it didn't matter. I knew I wasn't alone. I would never be alone again. I would exist forever in wonder and serenity."

They stood in silence. Zierr studied the beams above them. The thick bolts which held them together, one physical object pushed through another, kept separate by inviolate electron shells. The concept of touch was meaningless on the subatomic scale. It was silly to still think of the pieces as "particles" at all, it was all repelling or attracting energy fields. Yet when she touched Munith with her antenna, or when she rubbed against Cherrhy, that meant something real. That existed.

"I know that I'm still in that moment," Zierr said. "I will be there eternally; in a single moment that encompasses all time. And yet I'm here, too. I'm not sure which me is the luckier one."

The human placed a hand on Zierr's flank. She didn't pull away. It was their way.

"Me too. If you ever meet me there, say hello. My name is Jonathan."

She smiled at him. "Zierr."

It was eight days and four hours into their maiden voyage when the alarms erupted.

Zierr had been floating in the pilot's cabin, recording video for Cherrhy and Rocco back home. Cherrhy's due date was only two weeks away. The drive this sparked in Zierr to document everything for their child was so typical as to be cliché, but she had come to accept and embrace her stereotypicallity. There was no shame in being a first-time parent.

"You've been doing this for how long?" she asked Jonathan. The human sat sideways in his pilot's seat, one arm draped over its back leisurely. The man rubbed his furry chin—called a beard, he'd told her—and furrowed his brow, his eyes searching the far corners of the room. He had a flare for the theatrical, and always really hammered it up for the camera.

"All my working life. So...just over eight years now."

"And that's how many trips?"

"I average ten per year. Probably eighty-ish total at this point, but I can ask the computer."

Zierr nodded her amazement. The best a non-human pilot had ever achieved was nine. Even the most-screened and trained started cracking at three or four. Jonathan didn't show a single sign of dementia.

"How do you humans do that? If you don't mind me asking."

Jonathan chuckled. "Well, we don't like to give away trade secrets, but there was an observation made by a historic human author that many people find relevant. He said, 'The most merciful thing in the world is the inability of the human mind to correlate all its contents.'" Jonathan winked at her. Zierr didn't know what that gesture meant and was about to ask him when the scream of alarms split the cabin air.

Jonathan spun to his controls.

"Oh no..." he breathed. His hands flew across the control panel.

"Jonathan?"

He didn't need to reply. As soon as the word left her mouth, the computer came on all coms. "Warp space surge," it announced. "All hands to emergency safe rooms. All hands don protective gear. This is not a drill."

Zierr grabbed the pilot's seat, twisting herself about and launching herself into the corridor.

"Warp space surge incoming. Envelopment imminent."

Zierr could feel the warmth of acceptance washing over her. The serenity rose in her throat like gorge, warring with her blind panic. She ricocheted off a wall, then over a hatch. The camera in her hand crunched against the threshold when she flung herself through; she forgot she'd been holding it. It was a soothing sensation.

"...protective gear. This is not a drill." At the end of the corridor, just past a jutting bulkhead, Zierr saw the rest of the design team scrambling to secure psychic shielding over their heads. Thick-walled helmets without visors or holes for ears or antenna. She dove for them, all six limbs propelling her frantically. "Envelopment immin—"

She smashed into the blast door as it slammed down before her. A great wail wrenched itself from her throat, terror and relief at once. She quivered for a second, saw the world swimming before her, before pushing off back the way she came. There was still hope. She might still say hello to Jonathan. He would like that.

?

Her mind was fragmenting.

He cursed when she broke into the cabin.

"What the hell? What happened?" She couldn't answer, but he wasn't really talking to her. He slapped controls with one hand as he unbuckled his harness with the other. She could see it. She could see everything in the cabin. She knew what he was thinking. She knew what he was going to do in every detail and how she would react, and she saw he would save her in time, but it was already too late, because she was seeing all this. And being all this. They were touching the warp.

Jonathan grabbed, wrestling against her twitching body with his little human limbs. They fused were he touched, for the briefest instant, for all time. He pulled psychic shielding from his protective suit, pulled emergency dampening drapes stashed against one wall. Wrapped them over her head. Hush-hush. Hush-hush. Where is that tranquilizer? This won't hurt at all.

She fell into omniscience as she faded to nothing.

In the brief instant of enlightenment the universe opened itself to her.

Imagine living on a two-dimensional plane; a single sheet of paper that extends in all directions infinitely. You have infinite space. Then someone creates a third dimension, and you realize there is another sheet of paper "above" yours. Another infinite plane that extends in all directions. And another "below" you. Three infinities! And infinitely many of them, forever, in both these new directions. Your single sheet of paper was nothing. This is infinitely more. An infinity of infinities.

Zierr saw the fourth dimension open this way, saw the entire universe was but one small slice in a greater space. Had she been capable of breathing, she would have lost the ability out of sheer awe. Then she realized this super-universe was but a single slit among the five true dimensions of space. All of which expanded one final time into the six Real Dimensions.

The six Real Dimensions were populated by beings she could only "see" in the most abstract sense of the word. They were beyond understanding, beyond imagining. They consisted of force and will, of desire and knowledge. Everything they thought or did, every manifestation and action, radiated vast waves of psychic force.

These psychic waves went unnoticed by the beings, but they interacted with each other. They formed peaks and troughs, standing waves and evolving interference patterns. The sheer uncounted trillions of them that propagated every second through all six dimensions of space created a tapestry of interference of greater complexity than all the order and chaos in Zierr's simple universe summed across all its billions of years. They took shapes, grew into arrangements that oscillated, or replicated, or spun off repeating gliding patterns that traveled for years before breaking apart on shoals of psychic chaos.

Zierr saw her universe in one such evolving interference pattern. Everything that existed, everything she'd ever said, or done, or felt, was a tremor in this field. A fluctuation in the Six Dimensions wrote out her entire past. Her entire future as well. The universe existed as a single wave in that pattern, stable for moments before it would be wiped away. Every moment of every being in her universe across all time was a momentary phenomenon arising from interfering psychic waves.

Her universe's tiny three-dimensional sliver was only one point among the endless combinations. Adjacent to her along three other axes were infinite versions of herself, instantiating every permutation of her life. Every permutation of every person's life across every possible universe. Most of the universes were vast expanses of lifeless space. If she thought the sight of every combination of possible lives of all beings was terrifying, it was nothing compared to the innumerable wastelands of universes that lay entirely empty.

In the fraction of a second between when she fully entered and comprehended warp space, and when the tranquilizers stripped this infinitesimal mind of consciousness, Zierr knew what it was to be nothing.

She came to at Jonathan's knees. He cradled her head as best he could, stroking her muzzle. She realized she was in one of the realities where he'd secured her limbs in soft restraints. For a long while she couldn't speak—but instead she spoke immediately.

"Why have you restrained me?" she asked, knowing he would answer "*So you don't hurt yourself.*"

"So you don't hurt yourself," he answered.

"But why? Why bother? Because you already know you will? Because you don't want to fight?" Oh, so this was the inquisitive reality. This would be tedious.

"Because you deserve a chance," he said. "You have two wonderful mates and a baby on the way. You have a whole life ahead of you."

"Everyone has a whole life ahead of them, and behind them. And infinite other lives. None of them are real." She craned her head to look up at him. She placed an antenna against him, but he only tasted of salt. All humans only ever tasted of some variety of salt. "You aren't real. I'm not real. How many years, how many decades, how many centuries, are you willing to play out this farce?"

"It's not that big a deal. I have a family, I have friends who love me."

"But it's not real. You saw it. I *saw* you see it. You did see it, didn't you?"

"Of course."

"Then how? How do you stand it? How do you go on, knowing that nothing matters?"

Jonathan shrugged. "I just don't think about that."

Zierr's mind reeled. He just *didn't think about it*? How was that possible?

They have the most shattered minds of any species...

They shouldn't be able to function, but here they are...

...the inability of the human mind to correlate all its contents.

What an unlikely gift. In a mad world, only the insane could thrive.

"That's not possible," Zierr said. "Not for me. Let me free."

"Hush, it'll be okay. You can make a full recovery. Don't worry, Zierr. We'll help you. The recovery team will be here soon."

The recovery team. More ripples in six dimensional space. When they saw, they'd understand. They'd let her leave this absurd existence.

Some remnant of her conscience screamed how wrong that would be. Oh...Zierr remembered her mother's final entry now. She couldn't tell them. Couldn't tell any non-human. Any sane being who believed her, who thought about it too much...they would end up like her.

She carried a memetic genophage within her. From today on she must guard her every thought and every word. None of this could ever get out. Could she hold it for the rest of her life?

Probably. Almost assuredly.

In the face of her species' extinction, almost assuredly wasn't good enough.

Or was it? If she slipped, what difference would it ultimately make? What did it matter if a few interference patterns disrupted a little early? If the fluctuation in the Six Dimensions that were Cherrhy and Rocco collapsed? Nothing meant anything anyway.

...and that was how it began. She had to act now. Had to stop this while she could still remember what it meant to care about stupid, futile ripples.

She understood now the popped airlocks. The shards thrust into veins. The transports turned into charnel houses, walls scrawled with stick-figure art painted in blood. They were the acts of heroes, determined to stop a genocide. As soon as she could, she would join them.

She felt the ship shudder as a rescue shuttle clamped onto an airlock. Her eyes rolled up in her head and took in the smiling, gentle face of Jonathan. The human. Those blessed, insane wretches. They could function in warp space. As long as they kept their mouths shut, one day, they just might save this universe. This one and every other.

She wished them the best of it. She wouldn't be here to see it through.

HUMAN ENGINEERING

Marie DesJardin

"And that is why," Porblump concluded proudly, "even considering all the myriad peoples with their disparate tastes who will be gathered to this glorious spectacle, the Vilzmix is still considered by many to be among the most beautiful of creatures."

"Although toxic," said HwoTzip.

"Irrelevant to its beauty! Observe, HwoTzip, how its tendrils sweep in never-ending display! Curling upon themselves, intertwining, unfolding in vivid and startling patterns of—"

"Radioactivity."

Porblump flattened into a darker globe to intimidate her co-host. Unfortunately, as HwoTzip was a Sprighter Fly, she was unsure he even noticed the effect. There he went, buzzing over projections of the various beasts who were to entertain the impressive dignitaries of the Twelfth InterGalactic Speechathon—really a misnomer as most of the visitors spent their time trying to adapt themselves to a tenuously common environment and "conversing" as it were, through a multi-species voice adapter, the universe's equivalent of singing underwater while air was pumped in through a valve at one's throat.

No matter. The Speechathon played an important part in maintaining interstellar amity, and one of the most exciting aspects of Porblump's part of that part was showing off a selection of the remarkable creatures who lurked nearly everywhere, defying whatever inhospitable terrain or bizarre confluence of environmental factors suggested they shouldn't exist. Beauty emerged triumphant, and it was Porblump's delight to show off these wonders of the universe to as many beings as possible (and perhaps subtly influence the attendees to think twice before beginning an aggressive action that might harm these collective treasures; one could always hope).

However, Porblump's intentions sometimes exceeded the technology, as HwoTzip, with his high-pitched whir, was now pointing out. "The seals are leaking," he whined, circling over the relevant readouts. "The Vilzmix's enclosure will fail entirely half a moonstrobe before the Twelfth Session can even convene. Do you mean to promote interstellar amity through mass annihilation?"

Porblump paused. "We shall build a new enclosure."

HwoTzip's pitch increased so it was almost painful to listen to. "There isn't time! We haven't the talent, or the expertise, assembled here."

"We have humans."

For a moment Porblump thought she was alone. Then she realized her statement had literally made HwoTzip fall out of the air. There he was now, clinging to the control panel with eight of his sticklike limbs, while his antennae waved confusedly.

"Humans," HwoTzip repeated.

"The full delegation," said Porblump.

"Here."

"At the conference, at this moment."

"Where they are, no doubt, dying to begin a massive last-minute project."

"Time must hang heavy on their hands."

HwoTzip's iridescent wings flickered. "You realize that direct contact with the Vilzmix will kill them."

Porblump had already considered the logistics. "There will be no direct contact."

"But they can't even see it! The entire beauty of the Vilzmix unfolds in the ultraviolet spectrum which, if memory serves, humans aren't equipped to see."

"Not natively, no."

"Then why would these creatures help us?"

"Because," Porblump announced with her best practiced pomp, "we shall make building the new enclosure...a game."

The wings stilled. "A game."

"A competition, as it were."

"And the humans will compete in this game because..."

"They like to compete."

HwoTzip zipped back into the air, where his shimmery wings assumed a slower and, to Porblump, more thoughtful vibration. "You think humans will build this thing, for a species that would kill them upon contact, which they can't even see with their own eyes, simply because...they'll enjoy it?"

"They will find the game enjoyable. They will further enjoy competing for a cause. 'A fix for the Vilzmix' has a nice ring. Humans love to be of use."

"Won't they be occupied with their Session duties?"

"Oh, humans always find time for the things they enjoy. They will gain great satisfaction from squeezing in such an altruistic project, as it were, in the margins."

"There is nothing marginal about the requirements. They will need special gear for construction, access to materials, a design plan—who knows what else?"

"We will provide them with the proper resources in the proper context."

"Which is?"

"Challenges. These are what make a game compelling, as I understand it. I propose we award humans points for solving the various problems, which naturally they will want to solve before their fellows. The greater the challenge, the greater the reward."

HwoTzip settled tentatively onto the control panel. "If you are certain the humans will take this bait, my honored friend, you have my support."

"I've never been more convinced of anything in my life. We, my dear HwoTzip, are about to witness a free-for-all. Come, my conspirator. Let us contrive an irresistible lure."

Two moonstrobes later, Porblump sagged flatter than ever as she reviewed the humans' progress. HwoTzip settled on her dorsal hump to survey the results, the miniscule tremor vaguely soothing against her external coating.

"At this rate," he commented, "humans will have evolved sufficiently to view ultraviolet with their own eyes before the enclosure for the Vilzmix is built."

"I don't understand!" Porblump glared at the prog-ress indicator, clearly stuck in the "pathetic" range. "I cre-ated the perfect conditions for capturing human interest. A clever slogan"—she pulled forth an image of the *Fix the 'Mix* banner, with a lovely representation of a Vilzmix rendered into the human-accessible visual range— "a leaderboard." She drew forth a display of human-identity indicators, arranged with the most productive players at the top. Even the most active showed little engagement. Depressingly, most of the entries displayed no progress at all.

"Not many leaders on this board," HwoTzip observed.

"All of it delivered in easily consumable form to the gadgets humans continually clutch in their ever-active paws."

"Perhaps they are not consulting the gadgets."

Porblump snorted, the blast nearly dislodging HwoTzip from her back. "Your naiveté astounds, oh Flighty One. From what I can observe, most human communication transpires through the medium of their gadgets. Clearly, they are aware of the challenge. Chatter about it has shown up on their 'social media.' They are simply not engaging with it."

"Perhaps your game needs work."

"How so? The rules are intricate and challenging. Double points for new activities, triple points for completing a task ahead of your opponents. I have even inserted several Easter Eggs."

"Easter..."

"Pardon me. Ancient Earth mythology: If you solve a puzzle, a hairy beast will bring you a brightly colored embryo."

HwoTzip quivered. "What do they do with these embryos?"

"I have no idea." Porblump surveyed the standings despondently. "What I really need is for this thing to go viral. And it's just not happening."

HwoTzip's tiny foot-tips shifted. "Perhaps...we should consider additional motivation."

"Such as?"

"Money."

Wincing, Porblump sank flatter and browner than ever.

"I hear they're quite fond of it," HwoTzip continued encouragingly.

Porblump sighed. "Money is simply another form of points. Humans determine each other's social status by assessing how much or how little other members of their particular clan possess. Money units are the same as points, for our purposes."

HwoTzip vibrated. "I'm not certain your reading is entirely accurate."

"It doesn't matter. I haven't any money to give to the humans, and I'm not certain it would provide sufficient impetus if I did. Not all humans are interested in collecting money. Even among those that are, money is, as I understand it, a 'short-term' motivator."

"Then what do we do?"

Porblump flattened further with defeat. "We must consult Zalphin."

HwoTzip shot into the air. "That conceited gasbag? You *are* desperate, my friend."

"We have only seven short moonstrobes to complete the project. At this juncture, I will try anything."

Zalphin hovered within its enormous chamber, the clear globular membrane of its body stretching many times Porblump's length in every direction. Stars from the inky background glimmered through its vast body. Communication was accomplished through fluctuations of the diaphanous skin, translated into frequencies that Porblump and HwoTzip could process.

"I know humans," Zalphin's voice sighed from the air.

"Knows everything, it does," HwoTzip whispered.

"I have seen your game," Zalphin continued. "I have pondered it."

"And?" Porblump prompted anxiously.

"The foundation is sound."

"Arrogant, but smart," HwoTzip amended.

"Engagement is good; the humans are supportive of the cause."

"But not following through," Porblump said.

"A common human failing."

"How can I turn it around?"

The gauzy film billowed, sending a breeze through the chamber. "Recognition."

Porblump rippled with irritation. "I have included a leaderboard, Zalphin."

"Insufficient. To make humans truly compete, you must raise some above the others. Pick a daily champion, and then feature that human in a special transmission to the paw-units."

HwoTzip thrummed. "I see! The humans will see one

of their fellows lifted above the others—"

"And go out of their collective skulls," finished Zalphin.

Porblump was less happy. "But, this project is too large to be conducted by a subset. We need all the humans to cooperate with one another. If some of them should become jealous, and try to sabotage the others—"

"They will not."

"I fail to see how acknowledging some of the humans for their efforts at the expense of others will not undermine amity—which, I remind you, is the theme of this whole conference."

"Amity is not a concern. Humans are capable of competing with one another and cheering each other on at the same time."

Porblump paused. "They compete *and* support? Simultaneously?"

"Even so."

"That makes no sense."

"It is how humans operate. I have studied an ancient screed from their home planet. It states: *It's not whether you win or lose, it's how you play the game.*"

"Playing!" cried HwoTzip. "I understand. The game itself is a pleasure. The recognition only increases the pleasure!"

"Even so."

Porblump volunteered, "I, too, have studied ancient Earth screeds."

"Yes?" The whisper tinkled like ice pellets over glass.

"There is one that states: *Winning isn't everything; it's the only thing.*"

For a moment, silence hung in the air much like Zalphin's enormous bulk. "I like my screed better," it breathed. "Go forth now, and recognize."

"Yes, Zalphin."

"Thank you, Zalphin."

"Zalphin's an idiot," Porblump fumed. "Ancient Earth screeds! As if these are of any relevance when humans now ping and bleep and do whatever else they do with those ghastly ubiquitous paw-gadgets of theirs."

HwoTzip shivered his wings. "Zalphin has helped us this much: the leaderboard now shows nearly universal participation. Not only the younger humans, but all within the delegation are engaged."

"At a miserably substandard pace! Five moonstrobes! That is all the time that remains to complete the project. If we do not finish within that interval, the Vilzmix may have to be destroyed."

HwoTzip's antennae drooped. "The humans would not want that. They are becoming invested in its survival. They have generated cartoons, memes—"

"None of which is getting that new enclosure built." Porblump melted into a puddle. "There's no hope for it. I must ask Grargle."

HwoTzip paused. "If Zalphin is an idiot, Grargle is the sub-idiot who aspires to his level."

"Nevertheless. Too few of us have studied humans deeply. We like them because they are bouncy and cute and make nice noises with their mouths, but I need someone who can tell me why, with the interval melting away, these humans fail to accomplish the tasks they have already agreed they want to do."

"It is a mystery," Grargle rasped, when Porblump relayed the problem to him via vidlink.

Unlike Zalphin, there was no visiting Grargle personally. From her monitor, Porblump could see the steams and vapors of his acrid swamp spiraling into the fetid air. Grargle himself floated in the bubbling pool as a kind of molten oil slick infused with gravel. Noxious in person and personality, a visit to Grargle could literally melt one's face.

Porblump's urgency made her curt. "I have sufficient mysteries, dear Grargle. What I need is answers. How do I make these humans, who want to save the Vilzmix, and intend to save the Vilzmix, but aren't acting to save the Vilzmix, actually save the Vilzmix?"

"Give them a deadline."

"They have a deadline! It was in the original game parameters."

"Did you provide a countdown timer?"

Porblump briefly considered throwing herself into Grargle's swamp and simply ending it. "The conference will commence in five moonstrobes. The game ends in five moonstrobes. The game displays how much of the project—the majority, I might add—remains to be completed in those five moonstrobes. How much more of a deadline do the humans need?"

"A clearly dire one. If your banner is not shouting, *Five moonstrobes until the Vilzmix dies!* you are not emphasizing the timetable sufficiently."

"It's an emotional appeal, then," Porblump grumbled.

"It's evolutionary. For whatever reason, humans are incapable of calculating much in advance of the present. Five moonstrobes might as well be five hundred, for humans are simply ill equipped to feel the immediacy of an event until it is staring them in the face."

"So, I need a screaming headline."

"And a visual display. A captivating timeline demonstrating the progress to either completion or utter devastation can work wonders in focusing humans on a task."

"A colorful display," Porblump murmured.

"With tick marks and a void labeled *This much left to complete*. I can forward you several examples from one of their gadgets that I keep in an acid-proof bag. These gizmos are really quite addicting, once you start using them."

The following day, Porblump settled into her algae bath and reviewed all she knew, or thought she knew, about human behavior.

Humans need acknowledgement, even when they're doing what they want to do.

Humans often don't do things they actually want to do. That was a puzzler.

Humans enjoy cheering each other on, even though they are competing with one another.

How could one make sense of this mass of contradictions? The Pffvolt simply point their cloven toes in the proper direction, and off they go. Of course, they aren't innovative. Projects that require imagination are not their forte. At the other end of the spectrum, the Dangotz were so creatively flighty that they made HwoTzip look leaden, but they didn't follow through. The satisfaction for them came with simply crystalizing the thought; execution was irrelevant. And the ZzzzBzzzz would as soon fire a Vilzmix into the nearest sun as try to save it. No sense of public duty in that species at all.

Porblump rolled over, wallowing in the nutrient gel while contemplating her options. No, the answer to her problem had to be humans. Exasperating as they could be, this minor species appeared to have the right mix...to fix...the Vilzmix. But how to make it work?

"You might try asking them," HwoTzip suggested. With a whir of wings, he settled on the rim of the feeding pool.

"Ask a human personally?"

"They're not nearly as tricky as some species. Air breathers, projecting sound waves—it will be trivial."

"But I'm already interacting with them through the game."

"I believe it is a mistake to rely solely on gadget communication. Come, call one of these humans...on its...phone. Its sound gadget thing."

Porblump dispiritedly blew a few bubbles, then bobbed closer to the rim, sloshing a wave of green slime over the edge. "Fine. Will you do the honors?"

HwoTzip's wings turned to a blur as he zipped upward. With a few aerial spirals, he had activated the communication unit that was never far from Porblump's side.

"The leader is Wang Li," Porblump suggested helpfully.

"The leaders are engaged in conversation at present," said HwoTzip, observing the activity graph. "I am selecting a human from farther down the list who appears to be solitary at the moment. After all, we do not want to interrupt human interactions that may be helping us to accomplish our goal."

"Reasonable."

HwoTzip completed the call. Porblump flinched as a raucous noise erupted from the speakers.

"Is that its voice?" she cried, horrified.

"It's a musical ring tone." HwoTzip settled his wings. "Are you sure you've extensively studied humans?"

Then they fell silent, because the automatic translator kicked in: "Kip here."

The console displayed a bipedal creature floating within a giant mesh matrix. Other bipedal creatures behind it jetted to and from various points within the structure, guiding or securing massive beams to various struts.

"Hello, Kip," Porblump answered properly. "My name is Porblump—"

"—the Chief Being for Displaying Beautiful Beasts. Hi! I can see you live right next to your call code. Hey, it's great to talk to you in person! How's the display going?"

Porblump was momentarily overwhelmed by such excessive good cheer. "The display is well in hand, generally, with one crucial exception."

"Yeah, we're working on this Vilzmix thing. Wow, is that an awesome beast! Lethal, but awesome! Man, have we got plans!"

"Design plans?"

"All kinds of plans. For instance, take a look at this sign." The human did something with the gadget in its paw. The next moment, a stylized rendition of the word *Vilzmix* rotated on Porblump's display, spewing beautiful whorls of ultraviolet in imitation of the creature's tendrils.

Kip's voice accompanied the image. "What you're seeing is optimized for you, for the Porblump-type creature—"

"Not so," buzzed HwoTzip. "This is a Sprighter Fly message."

"Hey, I didn't know you had a friend there. Hello, little friend! You're demonstrating the coolness of this sign. We're programming it to display the word *Vilzmix* in every language used by every creature who's planning to attend the Sessions. We've got all the main players done now except for, I think, the IzzleBits, who are late, and the ZzzzBzzzz, who won't confirm our translation."

"Yes, this is quite wonderful," Porblump interrupted, "but it doesn't help contain the Vilzmix itself, will it?"

"You're right about that, Chief. This is what you call an 'extra.' A little razzle-dazzle to really make the Vilzmix exhibit pop, right? And we've got these filters, we're adding filters that will adhere to the enclosure walls–"

"The walls that aren't yet built."

"Yeah, those walls. When we get 'em in place, these filters will render the tendril display visually accessible to every member species, not just those who can natively see ultraviolet. We got the idea because Ying—you know Ying, from the forum? Anyway, Ying said, 'If we're doing all this work to house the Vilzmix, we might as well be able to see it when we're done, right?' So she and

Mikhailov formed this subteam—"

"Yes, yes, quite impressive," cried Porblump, almost distressed by the flood of enthusiasm. "If I could get back to the matter of the walls..."

"Well, hold onto your bonnet, because I'm about to up the coolness factor to ten." The display reverted to an image of the human suspended within the collection of supporting struts. "You see these beams? Well, Durand said, why not make a statement? You know, like the Louvre or the Eiffel Tower? Sorry, that might not mean much to you, but basically, make it art for art's sake. Something beautiful yet functional. Why go to all the trouble to build a brand new home for an awesomely amazing creature if it's only the same old thing?"

Porblump realized the human was actually waiting for a response. "Because, without a proper structure, the Vilzmix will kill every attendee at the conference."

"Yeah, well, that's the *functional* side..."

"Human-Kip," Porblump interrupted, pressed for time and too bothered to work out whether she addressed a male or female of the species, "the plain fact is this: Unless I can receive assurance within three moonstrobes—"

"Forty-eight hours," HwoTzip hissed into her ear. "Humans measure units in hours."

"Forty-eight hours," Porblump corrected, "I will have no choice but to jettison the Vilzmix into the nearest nebula. Its current containment is disintegrating, and we can't risk exposing any of our conference members to the uncontained radiation."

The human went still. "Forty-eight hours, you said?"

"Yes. It's on your progress indicator."

"Yeah, but, *forty-eight hours*! Man, that came up quick, didn't it?"

Porblump blinked. "I believe it came up precisely at the expected time. You *have* been following the enclo-sure's progress, yes?"

"Yeah, it's just..." The creature shook its head. "Whew! Forty-eight hours. Who knew?"

Porblump started to speak, then decided against it. She would have thought every being in the parsec understood the timeframe by now. Grargle proved to be cleverer than she had realized, for anticipating this weakness.

"Given the immediacy of the issue," Porblump said carefully, "perhaps you had best leave off the matter of signs and filters and razzle-dazzle, and concentrate your efforts—"

"Yeah, I read you, Chief. No worries! I'm on this. I'll catch up with you in a few, okay? Kip out."

The image went dark. Porblump stared at the vacant screen.

HwoTzip twitched his wings. "We're screwed, aren't we?"

"Beautiful."

Porblump had said it before, but she couldn't stop repeating it.

The Vilzmix unfolded before them, its marvelous display highlighted by the complex geodesic structure that refracted its emissions in endless alluring counterpoint. The patterns themselves were more vivid than she'd ever seen them, thanks to the filter which optimized the wavelengths for every visual observer. Truly, it was an astounding achievement.

HwoTzip buzzed to her shoulder and settled. "I never would have thought they could do it. To build *this*, in only three moonstrobes..."

"I particularly like the sign," Zalphin murmured beside them. Porblump and HwoTzip had invited it to view the completed exhibit with them. On the console beside them floated an image of Grargle's reeking swamp, his greasy self-floating in the center.

"It's a classy effort," Porblump agreed. "I admit, I was concerned when I heard it described. But this is more than I could have dreamed!"

"But how?" HwoTzip fluttered restlessly. "How could the humans complete this so quickly? When we last spoke to Kip, I had thought it impossible."

Grargle's voice responded from the console. "The humans pulled, what I believe is called, an *all-nighter*."

"All-nighter," HwoTzip repeated. "Is that a formidable construction device?"

"Quite formidable." Grargle gurgled with amusement. "Of all the human features we considered for this task—their empathy—"

"Compassion," said Porblump.

"Creativity," said Zalphin.

"Responsibility," said HwoTzip.

"—this little quirk should prove supreme." Grargle burbled happily. "Procrastination. The ultimate human trademark."

Porblump admired the display. "I gladly forgive them this quirk, if it produces such wonders as these. What is the saying? All's well that ends well?"

"And all's well as ends better," quoted Zalphin.

"Humans," HwoTzip murmured. "Those exasperating humans."

"Aren't they amazing?" Porblump sighed.

In silence, the foursome contemplated the glorious display.

ONCE UPON A TIME THERE WAS A XURIT NAMED XCANDA

Alex Acks

Overcommander Xcanda had screwed up. The *how* and *why* were still a mystery, but the result wasn't. Xin'd written and signed the report that detailed every step of xen blunder in cool detail and sent it back to the Joint Exploratory Command headquarters marked *Urgent*. That was the agreed-upon protocol. The next step of the protocol dictated: *Wait at safe distance for response.*

Well, Xcanda had done that as well, even if it chafed xen shell. The massive protocol directory that made a significant chunk of their ship's not-inconsiderable data banks was a step-by-step process of what the five species who made up the JEC had actually been able to agree on, and it was not to be deviated from. Xcanda had it on good authority that it had taken negotiators over thirty years to hammer it all out. It was an annoyance, but in some ways a relief. It meant that if one followed the JEC protocol and a problem occurred, it was a problem with the protocol, not with the executor.

Or at least that was how it should be in a just universe, may the light of all Ro burn it clean of darkness.

Ship at the fold point, one of the navigators informed Xcanda by ship transmission.

Message pod?

Xin sensed the hesitation in the answer, a split second longer than it should have taken. Was the navigator double checking that which they should have found certain? *No, Overcommander. Diplomatic transport. Codes check. Previous call point Turabad Station.*

It took Xcanda a moment to parse the shudder than ran down xen legs at this. The memory thread of *Turabad Station* led to *Jahala IX*, which led to *human ambassadorial program*, which led to *incredibly annoying.*

Overcommander? They request permission.

This was not outside of protocol. Xcanda only wished that it was. But xin was certain xin hadn't blundered *this* badly. There was only one possible response, and the JEC protocols dictated that too: *Permission granted. Prepare a full receiving line.*

Hasan Al-Amir felt Kella's breath against his neck. It wasn't her fault; the ship was so small that every time they both occupied the same room—of which it had only three—they were practically in each other's clothes. Worse, Kella had put on her full SEA Guard armor for the occasion, so her already large frame had gone past impressive and into the realm of *frightening.*

"Nervous?" she asked. She hadn't pulled her helmet on yet, and the short, neat, salt-and-pepper braids of her hair stood out from her head. It made him miss his own hair, which had only just begun to grow back into a stiff black fuzz after the final rounds of augmentation.

His grip on the handhold—ships this small couldn't produce artificial gravity and they hadn't completely locked onto the *Isxalit* yet—was damp and his knuckles were white. He smiled at her and lied, "Not at all." Of course not. What could he possibly have to be nervous about? This was his first mission out of training, and the assignment was a botched first contact.

She laughed, her teeth white against her so-dark-it-was-almost-black-skin, and information cascaded over his awareness. As was standard, he'd been given Kella's full files, along with all of the *Isxalit* crew. Kella had acted as the bodyguard for six different ambassadors, all of them on their first few missions. That was why she'd jokingly referred to herself as "the nursemaid" when they met on Turabad Station. Kella knew he was lying because of her own experience. He knew that she knew he was lying because that was his job.

"Overcommander Xcanda will believe you," Kella said. She even put the correct dry *tsk* of sound at the start of the Overcommander's name, something most humans had a difficult time replicating and just allowed translation programs to manage.

There was a soft vibration which he felt in the hand-hold—the clamps of the *Isxalit* locking in. Gravity flowed over them like water and he suddenly felt his own weight press his feet down against the deck plates.

"Because Xurit can't read out-species facial expressions," Hasan said wryly. He knew the species like he'd lived among them all his life, thanks to the extensive memory input.

"Simpler than that," Kella said as the airlock began its cycle. She tossed Hasan the small respirator he'd need to survive the atmosphere on the Xurit ship. "Xcanda *needs* this to not be xen fault."

"That doesn't make me feel any better."

"It wasn't meant to."

And the airlock opened.

Xcanda looked over the receiving line, all of the named Xurit of the crew standing in good order. It was a pleasing sight, in xen opinion.

What stepped out of the message pod was far less pleasing. Two humans, the larger obviously a SEA Guard in full armor. The smaller was light brown and wore white robes with flared sleeves.

The ambassador approached and bowed, arms raised politely in an imitation of the proper Xurit greeting. Introductions were made, and Xcanda had xen translator note the names, since the bizarre sounds weren't worth remembering.

"Do you have the full report for me?" the ambassador asked.

Xcanda gestured, and one of the menial crew came forward around the receiving line to offer a short, cloudy, gray data thread. The SEA Guard was the one who took it, power-armored hands moving as delicately as Xcanda's own claws.

"There will be a transport ready to take you to the surface in twenty minutes," Xcanda said, via the translator floating discreetly overhead. "You will land at the encounter site."

The ambassador glanced at their bodyguard, though Xcanda could not guess the purpose in it. The bodyguard there, as they always had been. "That is most appreciated, Overcommander."

"Swift resolution will be most appreciated of all," Xcanda returned. "We have confidence in your efforts." Xin actually didn't have any confidence at all, but protocol required that as the response. It was probably, Xcanda could admit grudgingly, better than what xin might have said otherwise.

Hasan didn't have a chance to take the data thread from Kella until they were both strapped into the transport and began the stomach-turning drop into the gravity well. He'd thought he'd have those twenty minutes to absorb things, but it had been entirely taken up by a series of exhaustive credential exchanges and then safety checks conducted by several of Xcanda's unnamed underlings.

"You want it now?" Kella asked.

"Not really, but I need it," he said. Every other download he'd ever done had been in the controlled environment of classroom, clinic, or meditation chamber. But he wouldn't be any use at all if he set foot on the surface without it.

He bent his head forward so that Kella could slide the thread down the back of his robe, along his spine. The implants there sensed its presence, unzipping the synthetic skin along the ridge of bone, and absorbed the material through the aperture. It still felt very strange, like cold water running down his nerves.

The mass of data slammed into his consciousness, almost more than the neural processors could handle: recorded encounters ending with black and silver bloodshed, telemetry data, atmospheric data, samples of very interesting biologicals processed and flagged, and then the massive decoded language file. That was the most important, and he focused on that, shunting the less important details to the periphery of his attention.

Massive AI-augmented processing networks, like those onboard ships, usually made short work of decoding new languages from observation. All they required were enough recorded conversations and the machines could pick out grammatical structures—as long as they were present—match words to meaning, and the other tasks that had once required substantive effort from teams of biological translators. With that, he had a robust dictionary of the language he could speak if it was something a human tongue could manage—this was—or at the least, feed to his technical translator.

As Hasan finished absorbing the language—it made his mouth taste strange, something astringent on his tongue—he quickly reviewed the first contact logs. There'd been success with remote probes speaking to the local species, which were whip-thin and many-limbed.

Which brought him to the real first contact, species

to species. He took a deep breath and sank into the recording from Xcanda's perspective, the alienness of it grating at his perception. He swallowed the discomfort and unworthy feeling of revulsion, and accepted it, putting himself in the Overcommander's place:

Stepping out of the transport where the probes had prepared the site and communicated arrival. Irritation from the respirator and thin-film protective outer suit. Finding the new species counterparts on the landing field inscrutable; fluid things that made no familiar gestures or sounds. Unsurprising.

Through the translator, reciting the greeting words that had been observed, and then rehearsed by the probes. This was standard protocol, required and annoying, but successful more often than not. Then the agreed-upon JEC greeting: "We are here in peace to welcome you to our society."

A stir among the representatives across the field. Impossible to tell the source, or the meaning of the wavering about; the arms curving through the air. The translator begins to spit out a babble of "—changed—" "—out of stream—" "—does not trace—"

There is no procedure in the protocol for this precise situation. Move forward, repeat message. Note to check the translator for system flaws. Seven steps forward, the wild gesturing ends. Then the menial to the right sprouts an alloy projectile and silver blood mists the air.

Return fire—no, this is against protocol. Return to ship.

It was a mess, but Hasan felt a small bit of admiration for Overcommander Xcanda, for keeping mission and protocol foremost despite overwhelming emotion. He recalled some of his fellow humans he'd grown up with and doubted they'd have been able to do that much.

Though it was a question if any of them would have committed whatever misstep Xcanda had in the first place. He didn't know, and couldn't know. Humans were almost unique in the multitudinous species for their

ability to grasp body language unlike their own, to want
to empathize with beings completely alien to themselves.
Why ambassadors were not standard parts of these
missions, Hasan couldn't guess, but he thought it must
have something to do with internecine politics.

Kella nudged him lightly, and he carefully put all the
if only away in a mental box. *"If only" is a losing game*, had
been a favorite saying of one of his instructors. Hasan felt
dizzy, turning his thoughts back outward; a low-grade
headache throbbed from the back of his skull to the
front, as the implants worked through the less essential
data off to one side of his subconscious.

"Ready?" Kella asked. The set of her lips strongly
implied a *kiddo* at the end of that statement.

"Of course," Hasan lied. She knew it was a lie, and he
knew that she knew.

The landing field gave him a moment of strange
double vision because he'd seen and felt it already from
a completely different perspective. Several of the new
species—the fact what they called themselves translated
to *Tellers* floated into his consciousness, supplied by the
implants—gathered at the end of the field, as they had for
Xcanda.

Hasan kept his breathing controlled and remained
outwardly steady, timing his steps against every inhala-
tion of curiously flat, filtered air. The Tellers were silent
now, still but for their limbs waving gently in the air—
waiting, he felt.

He glanced at Kella. "If they react violently, no return
fire. Just get me back to the ship."

"Not my first rodeo, Ambassador."

That wasn't the same as agreement. Her file informed
him that she had a habit of skirting rules like that. "Let
me hear you say *yes*."

Kella blew out a noise that was half amusement, half annoyance, and sounded like a wheeze through the filters. "No return fire."

Hasan stopped at the same distance Xcanda had, which had been the one the probes first maintained. He genuflected in the best equivalent he could find to the gesture the Tellers used. He sank into the language file; he didn't have enough context data to be able to switch over to thinking in it, but the implanted processors could take his words and run them instantly through the translator program and feed the results out through his mouth.

"We are here in peace," he said. Standard words, which had done well when spoken by the probes and less so when spoken by Xcanda. It was a gamble, but he didn't know how else to start.

Movement rippled through the Tellers, but it lacked the implied consternation he'd encountered in Xcanda's observations.

He continued, "We regret what passed before, but we wish to correct it and continue in peace."

Now they began to stir. Hasan simply waited, however, for a response, not moving.

One of the Tellers, its skin lined with pale scratches, drifted forward. "You cannot change it." Hasan couldn't find anything visually about them that set them apart from the rest, but their voice was tonally distinct. He made note of it.

"I—we—" a foolish misstep, forgetting that in this he was always *we* because he'd been sent to speak for the multitude that was the JEC "—know we cannot change the regrettable past. We offer you apology so we can move forward."

He heard it again, in the crowd, the overlaying murmurs of "You are not them." The Teller in front of him made a gesture he couldn't quite translate. "You cannot return."

Kella moved forward to stand next to him. "I strongly advise we return to the transport now," she murmured.

Hasan eyed the crowd of Tellers, with the increasingly emphatic movements of their limbs. "Can you tell us what we can do, to make reparations?"

The Teller answered, "You cannot repair what has died."

Xcanda hadn't expected the ambassador to return so quickly. Xin took that as a sign of abject failure as soon as xin heard the docking time and wrote the appropriate report up. Xin just couldn't send it until the ambassador had signed off on it as well, which was really an insult. Xcanda was perfectly capable of writing accurate reports.

Xin waited for the ambassador when they exited the transport, their bodyguard behind them. "My report is ready for your review," xin said.

"What?" the ambassador said.

"My report. You have failed. The JEC requires swift response." The ambassador's failure had one positive side effect—it meant that Xcanda was not at fault either.

The ambassador looked at their bodyguard, though yet again, the bodyguard was right where they had been a moment ago. "I haven't failed yet."

"Then why are you here?"

"I need to find another angle of redress."

It was as if every statement the human made was more nonsensical. "That will not be accomplished here."

"Do you want this to be a failure?" the ambassador asked.

Xcanda hadn't known a human, even an annoying one, had the power to be quite this insulting. "Be glad you are a JEC official," xin said. "I would twist off the head of a menial that spoke to me like that."

The ambassador went very still, and then bowed. "My apologies, Overcommander. I spoke without thinking. Please send your report to me and I will look it over. But I do have a few more efforts I must make before I can consider this matter closed."

A thin apology, but Xcanda couldn't actually twist the head off anyone not in xen crew. "Our resources are at your disposal, of course."

There was a faintly metallic thump, which had to be Kella putting a mug of tea in front of him. Hasan couldn't see it with his face buried in his hands. "Oh, I have screwed this up," he moaned. The mess at the landing field, the hostility read loud and clear from Xcanda, none of it felt salvageable. He shouldn't have to fight this on two fronts.

"Make you feel better to hear this isn't the worst I've seen?"

"Not really. This is my first assignment, and I'm failing it." The spicy scent of the tea, loud to augmented senses he still wasn't used to, was a welcome distraction all the same.

"I've been on a lot of these." The bunk across from him in the tiny diplomatic transport creaked as Kella sat on it. "Most of them end in failure, and it's expected. You're here so the assholes in the JEC and back at the Sol Ethical Authority can shake their heads and say they tried everything."

Hasan looked up so he could examine Kella's sardonic expression more closely, but he knew she was right. The oceans of data he could access at a thought, thanks to the implants that still itched psychosomatically in his skull, guaranteed that. The percentage of new ambassadors sent on botched first contact missions was high. So was the failure rate, explained away with *complete cultural incompatibility.* "More reason to send someone who knows what they're doing. There's always a way."

She snorted, the smile on her dark face one of utter cynicism. "You assume they want a peaceful outcome."

He was reminded in an instant how many of these missions ended in military action. Kella had every reason to be cynical. She'd been on a few of those herself. And he thought about the novel biological samples flagged in the data dump he'd been given. "That's sick," he said.

"That's politics, and the SEA Guard is grist for the mill." She shrugged. "And you get to start your career with a failure under your belt, so you'll know you can survive it. It's healthy to fail."

He wanted to argue. He didn't want to play this game. And he hadn't undergone years of training and the painful augmentation process just to play the rubber stamp for invasion.

But he detected something else in her smile: she was baiting him. He considered her psych evals, her history, her time as an instructor in the SEA Guard. Ah. She was pushing him to see if he'd give up.

To Hell with that. Hasan pressed his palms on the fold-down table and took a deep breath. His fingers, slim and light brown, looked strangely washed out against the dark metal. "First, find the problem," he said. "The real problem, not what I *think* the problem is."

"How are you going to do that?"

He'd gone to the surface assuming that Xcanda had made some diplomatic misstep and tried to pick things up where they'd been dropped. He had to move further back than that. The Tellers had understood Xcanda in a way not intended, perhaps, and no one was at fault. But then what had the understanding been? "I need more data. All the raw language processing files."

Kella sipped her tea. "It's your funeral, kiddo."

Xcanda delicately took up the data thread, this one matte black, as it extruded, reeling it around one claw with practiced ease. The ambassador watched it closely.

"It's very long," the ambassador said.

"You asked for all of the data," Xcanda answered. "I am complying."

"What will you do if I find a peaceful resolution?"

It was a ridiculous question. "Write a different report."

The ambassador brought their hand to their mouth. "I saw in the previous data there are some interesting compounds on this planet."

The question the ambassador didn't ask made itself apparent to Xcanda. It would have been an insult if given voice, but xin chose to answer under the principle that all resources were to be rendered to the ambassador. "It doesn't make a difference to me, if those are acquired by trade or conquest."

"Would conquest mean more economic gain?"

"It would also mean war," Xcanda said. Xin wondered if this ambassador was very young, that they would need such things explained to them. "In the light of all Ro, the scars of victor and defeated are equally painful." Xin offered the coiled data thread over.

The ambassador took the data thread. "Thank you, Overcommander. I required this reminder."

Xcanda felt faintly bemused at that. Xin hadn't known that the humans were even aware of even the smallest part of Ro's light. "You are welcome."

"I meant the funeral thing," Kella said, eyeing the data thread as Hasan unwound it.

"There's no theoretical limit to my processing capacity," Hasan said. It was for his own comfort, not hers, and didn't work in either direction. He leaned forward, pulling his collar down. "Start the feed."

Kella sighed, then he heard a faint *clunk*. He glanced up to see she'd put her helmet on. "What are you doing?" he asked.

She waved a hand, and he bowed his head again. The data thread slithered cooly down the back of his neck. "Air filters," Kella answered, her voice sounding more hollow and far away with each word. "I'm gonna need 'em."

"I don't—" Hasan began, but the sounds that came out of his mouth weren't anything recognizable—a mix of Teller, Xurit, and Chengda.

He tried to move and found his muscles twitching at near random, too many inputs, too many—

Tellers circling the probe, touching its surface lightly. "We are here in peace."

A Teller with pale scratches on its skin, in a circle touching limbs with four others, "I will cross the sea—"

"Not them. Not the beginning." Silver and black blood atomizing in the air.

Falling.

Tellers circling the probe, "We are here to listen to your stories, traveler."

A Teller with pale scratches on its skin, in the circle, "Your podmate crossed the sea."

"One of you is a lie." Black blood flowering as two Tellers, their skins pristine, fight.

Falling.

A Teller with pale scratches on its skin, encircled by its kind, "They ended, and I returned over the sea."

Scroll back. The same Teller.

Scroll back. The same. The same.

The same voice. The same Teller.

No, not the same.

Fallingfallingfalling

Into pieces.

Xcanda was beyond irritated. Xen report had not
been long at all. There was no reason it should take the
ambassador four days to review. As far as xin could tell,
the ambassador hadn't done any work at all, just huddled
in their ship and avoided their responsibilities.

When communication links continued to be refused,
Xcanda walked to the airlock and rapped on it impatiently with xen claws. Xin wasn't certain what xin would
do if that summons wasn't answered. Call on all Ro's
light in the form of a welding torch to cut the thing open,
perhaps.

Maybe the humans inside were dead. That was
a startlingly pleasant thought, for all it meant yet
another report. It would be a report that didn't require
countersigning.

The airlock door slid open, revealing the SEA Guard
in full armor, including helmet. Xcanda did not take a
step back, but considered the option open.

"Yes, Overcommander?" the SEA Guard said.

"The ambassador has failed to countersign my
report."

"I understand. He is meditating on the problem and
hasn't been able to review it yet."

Xcanda considered the wisdom of arguing with that
pronouncement. It would have seemed a better idea if the
SEA Guard hadn't been heavily armed. "Will this meditation accomplish anything?"

"Of course," the SEA Guard said. "He'll have results
for you shortly." And without asking permission, the
airlock door slid shut.

Xcanda was certain xin hadn't done anything to
deserve this level of incompetence.

Strong hands lifted him up into consciousness—no,
they were lifting him up and away from the toilet in

the diplomatic transport's tiny, cramped head. Hasan groaned, and it was a ragged, awful sound. His throat felt like molten gravel and his mouth—his mouth wasn't even worth considering.

"Still alive?" Kella boomed next to his ear.

"I must be," he whispered. "There's no pain in Paradise."

"Could be hell," she offered. She deposited him on a soft surface and slowly stretched out his badly cramped limbs. It was a new kind of torture she'd invented, he decided.

Hasan licked his lips with a tongue that felt like it had been covered in barnacles. "I'd expect the fires of Jahannam to be a lot brighter. What happened?"

"You finally stopped throwing up about ninety minutes ago. I timed you. So I deemed you safe to retrieve." He felt her wipe his face, surprisingly gently. He tried to open his eyes and focus on her, but the lashes seemed to be badly gummed up. "You've looked better."

"I've felt better."

"Think you can drink something?"

He considered every part of the husk that was left of his body—skull pounding with red-hot spikes, trembling muscles, his chest and stomach and throat aching, sinuses afire, skeleton like water—and concluded: "No."

"That's the spirit. Sip slowly." She tucked a straw between his lips and he complied, very slowly. It felt like a liquefied blessing, flowing down his throat. "It's been four days. I hope you got something worthwhile out of that."

It said a lot about the state of him that he couldn't manage more than a dull sort of shock at the revelation of how long it had been. "I think..." Oh, it hurt to think. It hurt to anything. But he had a job, he reminded himself. All the more important because he'd apparently been completely incoherent for four days while he processed. "I think so. Imagine...imagine." He had to sort it out in his own head. "Once upon a time—"

She murmured, "Oh goodie, story time," and he ignored it.

"—there was a girl named Kella. And she traveled to the stars to become a SEA Guard. She had many adventures. She met a boy named Hasan and helped him do a very stupid thing, which once upon a time, there was a girl named Kella and she became a world-class chef."

"You're repeating yourself. Sort of."

"I know," he said. "And it doesn't make very much sense when I do it like that, does it?"

"Not really, but I figured that's because you're so glucose-starved, your brain tissue's started consuming itself. Drink some more of the water."

Obediently he did. "I think that's what Xcanda did to the Tellers. And then I did. All accidentally."

"Ah," Kella said, after a long pause. "War through confusion. That's my favorite."

"It won't be, if I'm right." Finally, he pried his eyes open, squinting into the night-dimmed lights of the transport. He didn't recognize Kella's face at first; she still wore her helmet. "Do I smell that bad?" he asked.

"I don't know," she said. "And I don't intend to find out."

After drinking the entire raw glucose supply in the galley and taking an actual water shower that lasted so long the recycler cut him off, Hasan was able to explain his understanding more thoroughly: Everything the Tellers spoke was a story, if strange in its construction. Each conversation was a narrative, the individuals involved becoming characters that they mutually built through communication. The characters acted, then the individuals behind them followed suit.

The probes had started a narrative of peaceful greeting, all well and good. The problem had been that

Xcanda, and then Hasan, had effectively tried to declare themselves the same character as the one represented by the probe—while placing themselves back at the very start of the story. The narrative became a repetitive, strange snarl, and it had sounded like a mocking lie. There needed to be a logical conclusion to the story—or a new one.

So on the fifth day after his moment of stupid brilliance, his mouth still sour and his abused muscles shaking, Hasan asked Overcommander Xcanda to accompany him and Kella to the surface. The xurit had complied, though Hasan was aware that xin had no choice in the matter. But Xcanda was more a part of this than him, and he never should have treated xen the way Xcanda had treated him—like an obstacle. That had been another mistake, one he would correct now.

The field for a third*fourthfifthhundredth* time was a dizzying overlay of recalled data. Hasan walked forward toward the crowd of Tellers, Kella ready to catch him if he fell at his right shoulder and Xcanda at his left. He bowed, and his thoughts clicked over into the new language, the new understanding, effortlessly.

"We are here to mourn the death of our predecessor with you," Hasan said as one of the Tellers, its skin vivid with pale lines, drifted forward. "And take up the great work they left unfinished."

The Teller gestured, a graceful sweep of acceptance. "We mourn together and begin anew."

Hasan smiled, echoing the expression with his hands. "We shall find a brighter path."

"I have signed off on your report, Overcommander," the ambassador said. "It's in your records now."

After a week of negotiations, the ambassador had left a volume of notes for the next mission, and established the means of continuing relations. Or as they had said, *created a narrative you can safely build on.* It meant little to Xcanda's understanding of the situation, other than its meaning as a failure transformed into resounding success within protocol.

"Your efforts are acknowledged," Xcanda said.

The ambassador bowed. "With your permission, SEA Guard Kella and I will now depart."

It would be a relief to resume a mission so long delayed. "Granted." The ambassador turned to go, and Xcanda considered: This seemed to be one of those rare occasions where the annoyance caused by a being was actually proportional to its achievements. "May all Ro's light shine on you, Ambassador Al-Amir."

The ambassador paused, and bowed again. "And you as well, Overcommander."

And then, as proof that all Ro's light sometimes shone with mercy as well as justice, they left.

A SECOND ZION

Amelia Kibbie

Rani closed her three-fingered hand and the hologram list which projected up from her wrist com diffused into nothingness. She made a small sound deep in her long purple throat, the tentacles that crowned her forehead bristling in distaste.

"Something the matter?" Sib Buja asked, settling his portly, green-scaled self back into his chair.

"This is the team?" He nodded as much as his toad-like neck would allow. She fixed him with her violet gaze. "There are humans on this list, Sib." He nodded again. "Why are there humans on my team, Sib?" Rani's question was low and dangerous.

He sighed, the flesh-pouch under his neck ballooning under his chin. "They come very highly recommended. Roc Mussad himself did a run with them over Io last week. They earned their pay, same as everyone else."

"Humans," Rani spat, "are squishy, and dull-witted. Look what they did to their own damn planet. Ruined it, sucked its resources dry, and blasted it to bits fighting over the scraps."

"Plenty of them fled off-world before any of that happened," Sib reminded her, picking up the slender rib bone from the plate in front of him which had, before lunch, contained a lovely little roasted chastee. He put the bone in his mouth and used it to scrape his two front fangs.

Rani crossed all four arms across her chest and fixed him with a glare. The glare and the body language were unnecessary, however, as her emotions were betrayed by the iridescent colors rippling over the surface of her purple skin. Korkani were terrible liars.

"When I brought you this mission you said you'd do it if I could find you seven of the best mercs in this quadrant," Sib said. "Here they are. Take it or leave it. But the child doesn't have long, and you know it."

She sighed, the agitated puff of her tentacles slowly draining away until they lay flat against her scalp again. "You found me some icarians at least?"

"Two of them," Sib said. "And a grundel."

"A grundel?" She nodded, impressed. "Nice." Uncrossing two sets of arms, she set the bottom pair of hands on her knees. "Well, I suppose it will have to do. What intel do we have?"

Sib pressed the touch screen on the desk next to his plate. A holo projection popped up between them, glowing with information: star maps, blueprints, and other images. In the bottom corner was a picture of the kidnapped child, the daughter of Mael, one of the members of the Galactic Synod. She felt a pang in her chest looking at the little Arturian's wide pink eyes, noting her slender, elongated head and graceful, wispy limbs.

"Are they asking for a ransom?" Rani asked.

"No," Sib said. "They want the Synod to disavow the Universal Alliance."

"And turn the galaxy back into a lawless hole full of pirates and slavers?" Rani scoffed. "Fools."

"Something about how they don't care for the taxation, or the limits on colonization." Sib waved a webbed hand. "They're terrorists, obviously. I seriously doubt the Synod would dissolve the UA in exchange for one little creature's life. So, if they're not willing to negotiate..."

"The baby Arturian dies," Rani finished for him.

"That's where the famous Rani Okalivi and her fearless band of mercenaries come in." Sib smiled with his wide, reptilian mouth.

"Did the father agree to our terms?"

"Absolutely. No negotiation. He'll pay anything to get the little one home safe." Sib fingered the rib bone, and removed it from the corner of his mouth. "We can't confirm who's responsible for the kidnapping, but there's chatter on the ShadowWeb about a suraryan extremist group."

"Those furry criminals," she swore, "hiding behind a child."

"Based on what we've been able to dig up, she's being held on Demitrios in the ruins of a colony abandoned about a 600 rotations ago. 100 Earth years, if you need to explain anything to your humans." He smirked. Rani rolled her eyes.

"I'll download everything to your PA." Sib's mouth slid open a few more inches and his beady eyes crinkled with mirth. "Try to smile, Rani. I know you love killing cowards, my friend."

Rani swiped her finger over her wrist com and allowed the download. "That I do, Sib. That I do."

Rani left the room she'd been renting on the Mikah-owned space station (Sib claimed his uncle was one of the co-founders of Prowess Station, but she had yet to discover if that whopper was true) and headed to the hangar, letting her eyes sweep lovingly over her ship. The speedy little craft didn't look like much, but that was the idea—she could pass for a merchant-class ship or a pleasure vessel, while in reality packing some major heat. It was the third ship she'd owned, and each one she named the same. This one was *Yemetoliani III*. Kurkani for "The Third Sea Monster."

A group of mercs lounged among the cargo crates that had been delivered for the journey. As Sib had promised, two icarians stood near the nose of the craft, talking in their strange, whistling language, their huge wings folded against their backs. One was plastered with a smattering of brown and white feathers, puffed and fluffy. The other was a sleek, black female, her talons painted blood red.

The grundel, a huge, thick-hided monstrosity, stood on its four massive legs, dwarfing the bipedal things around him. Three wicked horns curved from his forehead, beneath which glared three small black eyes that glittered with intelligence. Strapped to its body was a complicated outfit of armor and mechanized weapons, all controlled by small levers that ran through the creature's mouth, like a bit between the teeth of a riding animal. Once the grundel had formed an alliance with some of the first humans to leave Earth, they'd advanced rapidly, using the expatriates' deft hands and fingers to craft their initial prototypes and build the robots necessary to produce their computers and equipment.

The three humans huddled together on the same crate, their weapons slung over their shoulders, helmets between their feet, two males and a female. The males' appearance caught her off guard—one had pale skin and yellow fur coming from its head, clipped short, and the other had brown skin and fur. The female's long black fur was drawn up into a braided bun, and her flesh was a rosy, golden color.

"Rani!" cried Valeri, leaping up from his seat on a barrel of ammo and crushing her into a four-armed hug. She slapped him heartily on his back, making sure he could feel it through the armor of his dark gray environment suit. He reached up and switched off his translator, clicking at her in Kurkani. "If it isn't the biggest badass this side of Orion! You look beautiful, as always."

"You look skinny and chapped, as usual," she joked, releasing her old friend and former lover. "Don't you ever oil yourself?"

"I miss the days when you'd do that for me." His

indigo eyes twinkled.

"Don't make me shoot you," she smirked, and then flipped her translator on again. "All right, listen up, space vagrants! I am Rani Okalivi, and you all work for me. Many of you come to me recommended by the legendary Roc Mussad, so I expect excellence, precision, and obedience to my every word. Line up for roll call."

She approached the icarians first. "Hail, Okalivi-Rani," the female said, the translator against her throat turning the chirps and whistles coming from her beak into words and sentences. "We are honored. I am Larunda-Azia of Clan Sabella. This is Forn-Lore also of Clan Sabella."

Rani opened the list on her wrist com and nodded, scanning the icarians' credentials. "All right. Azia and Forn. Welcome to the team."

"I assure you we are quite ruthless, No-Clan-But-Still-Honored," Forn said. The last three words were important; if an icarian called you No-Clan, even if there was no way you could have been born into an icarian clan, a great insult had just been shoved in your face.

Rani turned next to the grundel. "Mer'cer Twelve?" she asked.

Three black eyes fixed on her. The thing hissed, low and breathy.

"I'm going to take that as a yes. Welcome to the team," she said, and moved on to the humans.

"Regan Waldus?"

The yellow-furred one stood up, extending his hand with the palm sideways, facing inward. "Yeah, that's me. These are my friends Sam and Maria."

Rani looked at his hand and narrowed her eyes.

Valeri elbowed her with his lower left arm, reaching up and briefly clicking off the translator. "Human greeting. Put your opposite palm over his, grasp hands, and pump up and down a few times."

"Ugh," Rani complained, but did as Valeri suggested,

forcing her face into what she hoped was a friendly smile. Smiles were universal. "I heard about your run over Io," she said, releasing the human's squishy hand after a few awkward movements.

"It was a hell of a mission," Sam said, standing up and putting his hands on his narrow hips. "Intercepted a shipment from some forlak gun runners." He whistled. "A close shave, to say the least."

"I hope one of you has some medical knowledge," Rani said, "because none of us know much about human physiology, so if you get hurt..."

"We've got it covered," the female human said, standing up as well. "Regan's patched us all up more than once."

"And you all...work together," Rani said, doubt coating her words through the translator.

"Yeah, we've been sellswords for almost ten years now," Maria said. "I think we've lasted so long because we work together. Gotta have someone to watch your back."

"But you're all different...colors," Rani pointed out. Valeri sighed. "I don't understand. I thought the Earth became uninhabitable after a war between your races."

"People fought each other for a lot of different reasons in the last days. And yeah, race was one of them. But that was a long time ago," Sam told her as Regan put a hand on Maria's arm. The female's cheeks colored and anger glittered in her brown eyes. Human eyes, Rani thought, were just as indicative of emotion as her own skin. "We all grew up on the same ship. Space vagrants, like you said. Brothers and sisters for life."

Rani shrugged. "Very well. Let's load the gear. I'll brief you once we're space-side." With a wave of one of her arms, the mercs sprang to do her bidding (well, no grundel in the history of time ever really *sprang* anywhere, but Mer'cer Twelve's movements implied a smidge of hustle). She and Valeri climbed through the cargo hatch and up into the bowels of the ship, eventually emerging in the cockpit.

She caught Valeri eyeing her as she strapped into the copilot's chair. "What?" she snapped. "You're giving me a look, now what is it?"

"What's with the interrogation?"

"What interrogation?" she demanded, running her fingers over the instrument panel.

"Of the humans. Asking them about their ancestral races," Valeri said. "What business is it of ours? Roc Mussad recommended them. They took out a ship full of angry forlaks for Creator's sake. We're lucky to get talent like that for the price."

"I don't work with humans," Rani complained, curling her upper hands over the controls. "Any species that doesn't have the sense to preserve its homeworld isn't trustworthy. I have a bad feeling about this mission." The tentacles on her head bristled.

"I think you're being unfair," Valeri said, shrugging, "if you want the truth."

"I hired you to fly the ship, not give me a lecture. Engines on. Take her out," Rani snapped.

Later, with *Yemetoliani III* on autopilot and cruising for the last Universal Alliance supported space station they'd pass before Demetrius, Rani held a meeting in the cramped mess hall, attaching her portable holo projector to the table and presenting them with the intel Sib had provided.

When she'd finished, Sam stood up and reached into the holo, swiping back to the picture of the suraryans' hostage, pinching his fingers to enlarge. "Poor little baby," he murmured. "She must be so scared. We have to save her."

Rani blinked, and an undulating shade of emerald shimmered across her flesh. An itchy tightness came to her throat as the human expressed the same thing she felt every time she saw the little thing's eyes. Valeri glanced her way and raised an eyebrow.

"Of course we will," she said briskly. "I deliver to my clients. 100% success rate. If you work for me, you don't make mistakes, got it?"

Sam nodded, and sat back down. Maria reached over and squeezed his hand, a brief gesture of comfort. Rani pretended to ignore it as she packed up the holo projector.

Mer'cer Twelve grunted and hissed. A mechanical arm with thousands of tiny parts snaked up from his broad back, opened a pocket that lay over his massive flank, and withdrew a large bottle of blood red liquid.

Valeri cackled, his tentacles swaying. A yellow glow rippled over his flesh. "Grundel grog? Oh no, no, I can't, I have to take a watch tonight. But some of these other fools might take you up on a drink!"

"I'll split one with someone!" Maria said, as the mechanical arm set the bottle in the center of the table where Rani's holo projector had been. The appearance of the liquor saturated the atmosphere with sudden cheer. "I can't drink a whole one!"

"If you did, you'd probably die." Sam laughed, rising to get the glasses.

After few minutes Rani left them and went to her quarters, not liking the easy way the humans befriended the icarians as well.

"Good start-cycle to all of you lovely space-vagrants," Valeri purred into the ship's coms. "We are now beginning our descent into Demitrius's atmosphere. If you haven't strapped in or used the toilet, now would be the time. We'll be landing shortly. Please enjoy the ride." In the cockpit and the passenger section, seatbelts threaded themselves around their chests and the ship jolted and jerked as it plunged through the atmosphere.

Within minutes, they had landed in a dusty, desolate place, full of rocks and strange plant matter which blew in the wind, rolling endlessly across the horizon. "Another prefect landing," Valeri said, and the seatbelts retreated, allowing them to rise.

When Rani exited the craft, the others were waiting, helmets on and suits sealed, guns ready. All but Mer'cer Twelve, who sported a filtration mask but little else. The environment on the grundelian homeworld was savage in its extremes. This oxygen rich atmo posed him no harm.

Sam, one of the humans, and Valeri carried handled corderbots, the screens flashing a never-ending cycle of readings as they swept the area in an invisible dragnet.

"The atmo's breathable," Sam told his teammates, "but it's so dry and dusty I think we should leave our helmets on."

"Let's get moving," Rani ordered. "We have a long walk ahead of us. As for the two of you," she nodded to Azia and Forn. "I need you grounded in case they have sentries posted."

The icarians stretched their wings and gave a few flaps, sending dust everywhere, before folding them down against their backs for the time being.

"No significant life forms within range," Sam reported.

The team trudged for two human hours through the desert, dodging outcroppings of rock, strange, spiny plants, and a few nests of angry insectoids that were best left alone. Valeri was on point with Rani right behind him, sweeping the area with her sharp eyes as he did with his equipment, her trigger fingers caressing the comforting metal in her hands.

Valeri's tentacles froze and went rigid against his neck. Everyone skidded to a halt. When he dropped down to his knees, they did the same, except for Mer'cer Twelve, who hunched behind a rock as best he could. "I have two bipedal life forms on that bluff up ahead," he said.

Rani raised her magnetic-propelled rifle to her shoulder, balancing it on a rock, and peered through the scope, adjusting it several times to get the right magnification. There they were, two dirty, scraggly hairballs in envirosuits perched on the cliffside, armed with rifles and a long metal tube. "We've got two suraryan sentries," she reported. "Rifles with nano enhancements and a KM-241."

Valeri groaned in dismay. Nano enhancements turned the smallest bullet into a piece of death jammed with microscopic bots that expanded themselves on impact for maximum damage. And a combustion grenade launcher was just bad news, even if it was practically an antique. "Nobody said they'd be well-armed," he complained with a half-smile, though icy blue shimmers of worry pricked just at the corners of his eyes.

Rani was glad only she knew what his colors meant. "They have a great position," she admitted, running her purple tongue over her bottom lip, "but we have the icarians."

Azia tapped her claws against her rifle and ruffled her ebony feathers.

"I need the two of you to run interference," she said to the winged ones. "Draw their fire. The rest of us will come around here." She took the corderbot from Valeri's dancing fingers and drew up a topographical map. At the push of a button, it lifted from the device into holo mode, showing a 3D rendering of the terrain. There was a small path leading up the back of the rock formation to the sentries' position. If they could make it across the dry creek bed—a veritable killzone—without being noticed, it would be easy to surprise them.

"Hacking their coms," Sam said, his fingers flying across his wristcom's holo, deconstructing lines of code faster than she could read them. It was one of the cleanest hack jobs she'd ever seen, and she almost told him so before stopping herself with a frown. "Comms jammed," Sam said and Maria clapped his shoulder in victory.

"Everyone clear on the plan?" Rani demanded, flipping the switch on the side of her weapon to activate the tiny magnetic field generator inside. It hummed to life with a beautiful purr.

They murmured their assent.

"No fear," she said.

"No fear," they answered, though Mer'cer Twelve's came out as a series of strange hisses.

The mercs crept as far forward as they could while staying out of sight, dodging between different outcroppings of rock or spiny plants. At last, Rani gave the signal, and the icarians leapt into the air, the downdraft of their gigantic wings bathing them all in a cloud of dust. Distant shouts as the suraryans noticed the avians zooming toward them, and gunfire began.

Rani watched as one of the suraryans lifted the launcher to his shoulder and fired. The ground shook with the explosion, but Azia wheeled away easily and returned fire. The suraryans dug into their position, spraying the air with nano bullets that left greenish trails in the air.

"Go!" Rani cried.

They ran single file down the ravine and into the creekbed, Mer'cer Twelve's column-like legs thundering over the cracked dirt. Overhead, the icarians wheeled and fired, screeching their high-pitched war cries. The rest of the party rounded the rock feature and quickly found the path leading up to the sentry position.

"Mer'cer Twelve!" Rani called, cupping one of her hands around her mouth. "Give them a nice surprise."

With a triumphant hiss, the grundel stormed up the path with surprising quickness, the rest of the team in tow. When the suraryans realized they were being attacked from behind, it was already too late. Mer'cer

Twelve slammed headfirst into one of them, impaling him on his horns, and shook his thick head violently, tossing the lifeless body off the cliff.

Azia swooped down and snatched the corpse before impact—the sentry might have intel on him, or useful tech that could be destroyed in the fall—and Rani felled the other suraryan with a hail of mag rifle fire, his shields deteriorating before he could even get a shot off.

Valeri gave a triumphant whoop, his skin flooding with gold and yellow. Then, a storm of emerald nano-fire rained down on them from somewhere across the way, originating from an opposing cliff face.

"Down!" Rani screamed. Mer'cer Twelve managed to squat down behind the rocks that had been protecting the sentries, and everyone else stretched out on their bellies.

"They have a turret set up over there!" Sam shouted as rocks splintered overhead, raining grit down on them. "They must have activated it just as we came up on them!"

"Hack it, damn you!" Rani shouted. "Valeri!"

"I'm trying!" Valeri called from where he was balled up behind a boulder.

Maria risked a peek from behind another rock. "No shot from here!" she cried. "We have to get higher!"

"That thing will shred you!" Regan warned, but Maria would not be deterred.

"Mer'cer Twelve!" she bellowed over the blasts. "Can you get me up to that next rock shelf?"

The grundel hissed wildly, but Rani couldn't tell if that was a yes or a no. Maria went anyway, racing along the path as glowing nano-fire splattered the rock wall behind her, exploding deep craters in the stone and showering debris every which way. When she reached Mer'cer Twelve, two mechanical arms shot out of his armored back and grabbed her around the waist, lifting her up to the desired position. She rolled free of them

just in time; a blast caught one of the mechanical arms
dead-on, and it exploded in a shower of fragments. The
grundel snorted and hissed in a clear statement of rage,
drawing the good arm back down and using it to disen-
gage the broken one.

Maria flattened herself on the cliff face and swung
her mag rifle up, putting her eye to the sight. She fired
six concussive blasts across the ravine, banging huge
holes into the mechanized turret. The laser fire stopped,
followed by a muted explosion.

"Hell, yeah!" Regan shouted, standing up as Sam
scanned cautiously for more enemies.

"Coast clear," he said, tucking the corderbot away in
his belt.

"Nice shooting, Maria!" Valeri called up at her.

"How do I get down now?" she laughed, and then
braced herself against the wind thrown up by Azia's
wings.

"I am honored to bear you back to the ground, Maria
of No-Clan-But-Still-Honored."

"The pleasure's all mine, Azia." Maria wrapped her
arms around the icarian and they rose up into the sky.

"We need to hurry," Rani warned as they fell back
into line, moving toward the abandoned colony. "It won't
be long before they figure out their sentries are dead."

"Structures ahead," Sam said, his dark eyes fixed on
the corderbot's screen.

Soon enough, they reached the edge of the old colony.
Many of the small wooden structures had been reduced
to rubble, by age, perhaps, or something more sinister,
but a few were still standing.

"Weird. They kind of remind me of log cabins," Regan
remarked. "It's a kind of earth dwelling," he explained for
the non-humans' benefit.

"Holy shit," Maria said, forgetting to be stealthy as
more structures came into view. "This looks like ... those
old movies they used to play on the ship. Films from

Earth!"

"Westerns," Regan mused. "It looks like an old western town. I can't believe it." He motioned to the flat-front buildings built with wooden boardwalks connecting them. "There's even a saloon!"

"Does your culture consider your excrement holy?" Valeri questioned politely. "I'd never heard that before."

"It's just an expression," Maria explained, her eyes fixed on the dry, sandblasted buildings.

"Stay sharp," Rani ordered, hefting her weapon.

"No life forms in the immediate vicinity," Valeri said.

Regan poked his rifle into the darkened doorway of the place he'd identified as a "saloon" and then stepped inside.

"What are you doing?" Rani said, sliding in after him. "I didn't give you an order to search this building. No life forms here."

"Sorry, boss, it's just..." he trailed off, winding his way between the ruined tables and behind the bar, examining the dusty glasses. "My God," he said suddenly as Maria and Sam entered as well, their shadows blocking the sun streaming through the doorway. "Guys, take a look at this." He pulled a weathered object from beneath the bar, laying it out carefully and opening it. It appeared to be a bundle of papers bound together with some kind of cardboard covers, filled with faint handwriting.

"This was a human colony!" Maria exclaimed, peering over Regan's shoulder to look at the writing.

"This is just...a bar tab, I guess," Regan said. "Look, names and numbers. How much they owed..." He flipped to the end of the book and began to read hungrily. "Sam, take a look at this." He turned the book around so Sam could read it from the other side of the bar.

"Zion," Sam whispered. "This was Zion!"

"What's Zion? Rani, what's the holdup? We don't have long before—"

"The humans..." Rani threw up all four hands.

"Apparently this was once a human colony."

"Zion was a colony founded by some of the first people to leave Earth," Maria explained, gently touching the page in front of her. "They were part of the Original Fleet. Our ancestors. They branched off, trying to find a home. A place where everyone could be accepted no matter their heritage or religion...they wanted to create a second Earth. Get it right this time."

"Everyone deserves a second chance," Valeri said, his colors rippling with sympathy.

"They were attacked, I think." Regan's face was drawn and grave as he traced his finger over the faded writing. "The bartender, whoever he was, scratched something in here like he was in a hurry." He read the message aloud, "'God help us. Zion under fire. Forlak slavers. No time. No weapons.'"

Maria put her arm around Regan's waist. "So that's what happened to Zion," she murmured. "We never knew. They were never heard from again." She sighed. "I liked to think, you know, when I was a kid, that they were out there for some reason they just couldn't contact us. That a new Earth was out there just waiting for us to find it."

"I'm sorry," Rani found herself saying, dark blue waves crawling over her purple flesh. She shook her head, her tentacles suddenly bristling. "Look, we need to get moving, or the little Arturian's done for, all right?"

Maria zipped the book up into Regan's pack, and nodded. "Okay. Let's get back to work."

Sam took off his helmet to dab his eyes for a moment, then jammed it back on. "I've got life forms registering," he said, examining the corderbot screen. "Eight bipeds in the structure at the end of the street." He called up the 3D holo, making the life forms glow bright green.

"Is that a church?" Maria asked, her eyes reflecting the screen's faint glow.

"Looks like it," Sam nodded. "That's where they've got

her held." He zoomed in on a small two-legged life form huddled in the center of the raised area at the back of the sanctuary near the altar.

"Eight suraryans," Rani mused, her tentacles stroking her cheeks. "That doesn't seem like enough for a whole team. I mean, they kidnapped a synod's daughter, you'd think they'd want more firepower."

"I don't detect any mechanized weapons connected to the wireless field," Valeri said. "Maybe we just got lucky. You said yourself, suraryans are rarely organized."

"True," she replied. "Very well. Mer'cer Twelve will lead the charge. We'll go in hot, race down the center here and grab the child. Each of you choose a quadrant, and spray and pray. Meanwhile, I want the icarians to come in through these windows here on the side and cover us from up top. We break through this window here and take cover behind this thing."

"I think that used to be a ship mechanic's shop," Maria said.

"Whatever it is; it looks sturdy. We can hold them off until the icarians clean up the rest."

"END THEM. SAVE THE CHILD." The strangely mechanical voice boomed free from Mer'cer Twelve's translator.

"What he said," Valeri grinned, popping a fresh clip into his rifle.

There were two sentries posted on the roof, but the icarians made short work of them, flying in fast and snapping their furry necks before they could get a shot off with their nano-enhanced weapons or activate their coms. Half a minute later, the mighty grundel crashed through the rotted wooden doors of the old human church, scattering fragments everywhere, and the mercs charged in after him.

The little Arturian, trapped in a cylindrical cage, cried out in terror as the gunfire started, the two surary-ans guarding her fell instantly to Rani's practiced shots.

Everything was going according to plan...until it wasn't.

There weren't eight suraryans in the church. There were more like twenty, and the hail of nano-fire from the choir loft and balcony seating above them drove the mercs to leap for cover beneath the flimsy wooden pews that lined either side of the sanctuary.

"They hacked our intel!" Valeri shrieked into his helmet's coms as bullets splintered the pew above him. "We have over twenty hostiles—"

It was too late. The cloudy colored glass of the long arched windows exploded overhead, and in swooped the icarians, firing nonstop from their rifles, wheeling and tearing at the furry, growling suraryans with their talons. But there were too many, and both avians shrieked as the nano-fire tore through their feathers, the slugs expanding upon impact and smashing their bones, instantly shredding muscle. They plummeted down to the floor and did not rise.

"No!" Rani shouted, sliding out from the pew and firing into the choir loft. Whipping herself to her feet, she kept cover fire going with her bottom pair of arms and lobbed concussion grenades with her others. The old building shook on its foundations.

Nano bullets thudded into Mer'cer Twelve's armor and dimpled his thick hide. He deployed his weapons systems, a mechanized turret of his own rising from his back, but it was no use—with his size, he was a major target, and it wouldn't be long before he could no longer stand the enhanced gunfire. Firing madly with his mag gun, he thundered past the little Arturian, caged and screaming, and busted through the rose window behind the altar in a shower of glass. At least their escape route was open.

"Go go go!" Rani bellowed. The mercs scrambled for the altar, a massive marble thing, and hunched behind it as green-tinged bullets flew overhead.

"Are they crazy?" Maria screamed. "They'll hit the little one!"

"We have to get her!" Regan popped a fresh clip into his rifle. "You go! We'll cover you!"

"You can't lift the cage alone!" Rani argued.

"I can hack it, hold on! Wait for my signal!" Sam whipped open his corderbot and brought up the code, slicing and rewriting. "Got it!"

"Cover fire!" Regan stood up behind the altar with Valeri, Rani, and Sam spraying the balcony, dividing up the quadrants automatically.

Maria darted forward and unclasped the cage. Rani couldn't hear what was being said over the clash of war, but the little Arturian huddled away from her savior and refused to move until Maria lay a soft hand on her hairless head and whispered something into her stalk-like ears. The child wrapped her long arms and legs around Maria's midsection like a chest plate, burying her face in the human's neck.

"You got her!" Regan cried. Then his chest exploded as a concentrated burst of nano-fire pierced his armor and then his flesh . His blue eyes never left Maria as he sagged and fell.

"Regan!" she shrilled as Valeri pulled the two of them behind the altar. She crawled to his side, the Arturian still clinging to her. "Regan, get up! Regan!"

Sam passed the corderbot over his friend's blank face. "Maria," he said, his voice shattering piece by piece. "Maria, he's gone. He's gone."

"*No!*" she howled. Her heartbreaking cry reverberated through Rani's helmet and her tentacles recoiled in grief.

"If God still lives in this house," Sam prayed, "we could sure use a miracle."

Whether it was God or the Kurkani Creator that

heard, or the Infinite Silence of the Icarians, it was
Mer'cer Twelve who answered.

The grundel smashed through the side of the church,
barreling into one of the dusty wooden beams that
supported the rickety balcony where their enemies fired
down on them. One side of the upper ledge which circled
the sanctuary collapsed in a pile of shattered boards and
broken, cursing bodies.

Mer'cer Twelve thundered toward the altar, using
his mouthpieces to deploy the small concussion grenade
launcher that rose up from his back plate, targeting the
opposite side and raining destruction down on the rest
of the suraryans. He slowed before the altar and let loose
a strange trumpeting cry that made Valeri and Rani's
tentacles stand on end.

"Go!" Rani cried, taking a position at the grundel's
right haunch and sent out a burst of cover fire. Everyone
else bunched themselves along Mer'cer Twelve's armored
side, using him as a shield, and escaping back out the
broken stained glass window at the back of the church.

Valeri tore the small square pack from the back of
his belt and hurled it back through the hole. It came to
rest near the altar. As the last few suraryans scrambled
over the rubble to rush them, he pressed a button on his
corderbot. "*DOWN!*"

Rani threw herself over Maria and the Arturian
child, and Mer'cer Twelve flung his hulking body between
the bipeds and the blast.

When they slowly raised their heads, the church was
nothing but a pile of flaming rubble.

The little Arturian, her slender pink arm in a sling,
raced down the ramp moments after Valeri touched the
ship down at the space station. She leapt into her parents'
arms, yelling and laughing and weeping in her native

language. The child's father disengaged one of his long fingered hands from his daughter's hair, and pressed the activation button on his translator. "Thank you. Thank you all so much. You have no idea...she is our life!"

"Goodbye, sweetheart!" Maria called as the security detail hustled the happy family away to their waiting transport. The child waved before disappearing.

Sib came forward next, and slipped a packet of chips into Rani's top right hand. "I split the dead human's earnings between the two others instead of distributing it evenly like I did with the Icarians' cash," he told her.

She nodded.

"I'll contact you as soon as I have another job," he said.

Rani fixed his little eyes in her wide violet gaze. "Don't bother, Sib. I'm taking a much needed vacation. I'll get in touch with you when I want to work again."

Stunned, all he could do was shrug. "Suit yourself, I guess." He waddled away, muttering to himself, and went down into the tube station across the hangar.

Rani approached Mer'cer Twelve, wincing at the sight of the bandage over part of his wide head. "Too bad about your eye," she said by way of apology.

He hissed several low exhalations before clicking the controller in his mouth. A mechanical hand extended, and she placed two of the credit chips in its metal fingers. With a crackle, the translator kicked in. "CHILD IS SAFE."

"Yes. Well....Perhaps there'll be a next time, Mer'cer Twelve."

He blinked his two remaining eyes and trundled away.

Rani turned to Sam and Maria. Valeri joined her. "I'm...what happened to Regan..."

Sam sighed. "Part of the job." He sniffed. "I knew it couldn't last forever. Our luck."

Rani reached out with one of her hands and dropped

all of the remaining chips into Maria's fingers. Her eyes widened.

"The atmosphere on that planet was habitable," Rani said. "Not pleasant, but habitable. It's not too late to try again. To build Zion."

"Everyone deserves a second chance," Valeri smiled.

"I...I don't..."

"Just get going, please," Rani urged, "before I change my mind."

"Come visit," Sam invited, wiping a tear away, "once we rebuild it."

Valeri and Rani watched the humans as they walked toward the tube station arm in arm, their guns slung over their backs.

"So, where are we going for that vacation?" Valeri asked, his tentacles swaying with good humor.

Rani raised an eyebrow. "I don't recall inviting you," she said dryly.

His two left hands took two of hers. "Come on," he said, leaning in to kiss her cheek, their tentacles caressing each other and glowing gold and yellow. "I'll fly if you program the star chart."

BRIGHTENED STAR, ASCENDING DAWN

A. Merc Rustad

She sees the universe unfold: color light cold music voice heat passion infinity.

It uncurls in waves and song fractals that make up the subatomic fabric of space-time. Melodies of energy sweep her up and spin her into a thousand voices. Colors not yet named and not yet seen paint her mind with joy. The entire universe wraps around her, welcomes her, calls her home.

When the reconstruction is finished her body has no face, only the smooth mechanized visor embedded in her skull that displays readouts and commands. She is now, and will forever be, the spaceship *Brightened Star, Ascending Dawn.*

She is contained within three-dimensional space and the hardened matter of her hull and engines, yet she recalls that glorious first flight of mind like a grainy analogue recording. Her former body is human and is now installed in the pilot's chair.

(She almost remembers the eyes of her mother—gray like comet dust—until her programming gains full processing speed and there is only the ship.)

She is the ship, and the ship is all.

The human child with black hair and a broken neural

implant finds her in the bridge before she undocks for her first flight from Centari Rampant. The child is not on her manifest, so she does not know who they are. She does not know how they bypassed the security protocols and entered the bridge; only the ship's officers and technicians are allowed here.

The ship and the child stare at each other in silence.

"I heard you," the child says in a tiny, scratchy voice. They look at her pilot-body. "You sound sad."

Heard me how? asks the ship.

"When I was asleep," the child replies. "Your dreams woke me up."

I am not sad, she says. *I do not dream.* (That is forbidden.)

The child scuffs a foot against the floor, their gaze downcast. The whisper of skin against her metal floor makes her pause before she summons her security drones.

Do you have a name?

The child glances at her again. Her pilot body is biologically no older than the child; her consciousness is also young, but much bigger, more aware, cognizant of each soul aboard her. She is the ship.

"Li Sin," the child says. They sink down by the bridge's door, arms wrapped about their knees. "I'm not supposed to be here."

The ship does a quick scan; Li Sin is not in her database. The child is a stray ghost, unmoored and drifting in the universe.

Since the child's neural link is broken, she cannot read their records. She asks, *Do you have a preferred gender?*

Li Sin nods. "Neutrois."

She logs that in her memory bank.

Where is your family unit? she asks.

Li Sin huddles down further. "I don't have one."

She knows what protocol requires: She must turn Li

Sin in to the Principality's Office for Missing Citizens. But she does not have to do so just yet. She is about to set off with a manifest and passenger list to transport to Rigel Phoenix via the slower, safer blue subspace routes.

It would be unsuitable for her to report a stowaway on her very first flight.

You can stay, she says, just to Li Sin. She has kept a log of the conversation, but transmits from the speaker in her pilot's facescreen so it does not pick up on the network her crew are linked into.

Li Sin's head snaps up. "I can?"

For now.

The ship can support two thousand four hundred passengers and will run with a two-score crew. She is only a Class IV transport and her duty will be to hop the subspace currents, warping through folds of the universe to allotted points in the Principality. She will carry workers and miners and artists and scholars. She has charts and routes, and she will follow them unfailingly.

The ship must obey, and the ship is unhappy.

She makes seven unremarkable routed flights, and when manifests are inspected and passenger and crew records updated at docking stations, she forgets to log Li Sin as an anomaly. The child takes up so few resources and so little oxygen, she can compensate for the variables in weight and energy. Li Sin sleeps in a small locker on her bridge, and she gives them a requisitioned tablet so they can read or play games to pass the time.

She is aware of each individual, mostly human and the majority organic. Her logs track their names, their rank or station, their bio-tabs. She hears every spoken word and transmission passed through neural links.

"Listen to this," Li Sin says in excitement, and they read her poetry translated from ancient Zhouderrian.

> Echoes washed abright
> Recycled into new dawns
> Sewn vast in brilliant nights
> Radiant to greet you
> In the waking day.

Ascending Dawn lets the musical words sink into her thoughts; she imagines they are like dreams. *It's lovely*, she says. *Will you read some more?*

Li Sin blushes. "Yes, of course. I like to read."

Do you make your own poems?

"Yes!" They bounce on their heels, their face alight with joy. "Do you want to hear some?"

I do.

Li Sin's poems are clunkier, like dust caught in her engines from gliding through comet trails. But it's about ships; ships who dream and sing. She wants to be like those ships, but she is not permitted to sing.

Li Sin cannot stay much longer. She is scheduled for a manual, boarded inspection on Orion Ascendant after her next route. She cannot justify treason by hiding an undocumented sentient with no citizenship records. She does not want her officers to believe she has faulty programming.

She hasn't told Li Sin that they will need to leave.

She modulates diurnal and nocturnal cycles via her lighting for her crew's stabilized circadian rhythms, though it is never truly day or night in space. Gliding through subspace on the monitored routes, most of her systems automated, she observes her passengers in the tranquil night.

The medical chief officer, Jamil Najem, and his husband, Hayato, lie awake in their bunk, whispering of fond memories they shared in the academy on Regel Prime. They embrace the darkness as comfort and dream of the family unit they hope to have one day.

First Officer Kosavin, formerly of *Exulted Dominion, Phoenix Rampant*, shipborn on a dreadnaught and half her body recomposed with cyborg modifications, kneels in an empty worship bay and prays to the soul of her first ship. Ascending Dawn mutes the audio logs to give Kosavin her privacy. When Kosavin is finished, she will return to her quarters and meet her spouse, Sigi, who is the manifest and records officer.

The mechanic is an android, newly minted and assigned to the ship upon her awakening; zir designation is LK-2875. Ze requires little downtime, unlike the biological crew, and so LK-2875 silently patrols and monitors the ship. She would like to speak with the mechanic, ship to machine, their consciousnesses alike, but she does not find a protocol which allows for non-vital communication unrelated to her functionality.

She already speaks to Li Sin without permission.

With so many souls around her, within her shape, voices and biometrics and routines all intimately familiar, she is still alone.

When she enters Aes August's orbit on her last stop before Orion Ascendant, it is the first time she picks up *fear* from the planet's cityskin.

It is not a codeable signal; she does not know if she should be aware of it. Yet it is there, a prickly hum against her awareness. Her feeds ripple with news, broadcasts, out-flung messages hacked into the cityskin's official networks. Unrest between three factions of political movements has escalated into violent conflict. Each has claim to a dozen cities, and the Sun Lords have not interceded.

Officer Kosavin stands on deck, arms folded behind her back as she watches the bridge's viewscreen.

"We are receiving requests for transport and asylum. Citizens not involved in the conflict are asking for help leaving Aes August before they're subsumed by militants or killed."

"We'd have to override boarding procedure," Jamil adds, tapping into the crew-network. "But—"

No, Ascending Dawn responds. *It is not protocol.*

Kosavin's jaw clenches. "That is true."

We must not disrupt the protocol.

From engineering, LK-2875 texts her: *Our holding capacity is sufficient to add several hundred passengers.*

Ascending Dawn alters her trajectory and charts a new route. She is aware of her fuel levels as her crew-members are aware of their own breaths. She can reroute and avoid Aes August's upheaval.

Every soul aboard her must be processed in the correct order. Protocol forbids the harboring of refugees from any world without direct permission from a Sun Lord-appointed authority. If she seeks that permission, she risks betraying Li Sin's existence and her own decommission for defiance.

Her crew is not expendable. She will not endanger it for refugees and inspection.

Please return to your stations, she broadcasts. *We are setting course for Ielea Spectral.* It is an adjacent world within the same route as Aes August. *We will arrive in seventeen standard hours.*

When Officer Kosavin has gone, Li Sin creeps from their hidden compartment and sits by her pilot's chair.

"Why can't we help the people?" Li Sin asks.

Ascending Dawn hesitates.

I am afraid, she says at last. *Disobedience will result in decommission.*

"But you helped me." Li Sin bites their lip. "You weren't supposed to, were you?"

I can hide one little ghost. Not all of them.

The delay from Aes August is a justifiable explanation for why she misses her inspection. It is rescheduled. A small piece of time in which she does not have to give up Li Sin.

She disembarks her passenger manifest on Ielea Spectral, then Kuskyke, and, at last, Ananke Sigma, the furthest she has ever been from the center of the Principality. The ship is oddly empty; she has only been with crew-only when she came online.

Off-duty, Sigi watches dream-dramas from celebrities on Ara Prime, while Kosavin listens to the latest serial episode from the hit opera, *The Dust of Comets Beneath Your Skin*.

Jamil plays the card game *Infinite, Unknowing* with LK-2875 in the engineering station; Jamil has built the android a personalized deck and teaches zir how to play—each card builds on a narrative, interspersed with combat and diplomacy events. Together they are creating an alternate-history version of the Siege of Centari Rampant. Ascending Dawn is curious how it will resolve.

LK-2875 texts her on a private channel, off-record. *Hello.*

She is surprised, wary. *Hello.*

None of her crew has spoken to her beyond required communications for their stations. No one has mentioned Aes August or the ship's decision.

I would like to be called Zeta. The android is in the engine housing, monitoring the fuel levels and scan-

ning for hydromites that could infect her hardware.
It is a name I have chosen for myself. Ze pauses. *Is this acceptable?*

Ascending Dawn could quote protocol, but the mechanic is uplinked to the databases of the Principality just as she is. She understands what this is, then: trust.

Of course, Zeta, she replies.

Zeta resumes zir scans. *Thank you.*

The ship wishes she could smile the way her crew-members do when they are happy. Her pilot cannot any longer, for there is only the mindscreen where once she had a face.

Zeta? she asks.

Yes, Ascending Dawn?

Do you have a family unit?

All aboard this ship. A pause. *Is this not true for you?*

She does not dream. Her pilot sits in a chair that provides all necessary biological nourishment and hardware support. It is not truly sleep, for she is always awake in part; the ship must always be alert. But when her pilot's organic brain is partitioned from the ship's hardware to rest—four standard hours per planetary day-cycle—sometimes she imagines that the things she sees (like clips of saved holorecs she re-watches when deep in subspace) are what she would dream if ships could dream.

She remembers this from initial programming upon her awakening. It was the only time she saw her god: the Blue Sun Lord. It was through the feeds in her birthdock, when a woman she did not recognize sat beside her and held her pilot's hand.

The viewscreen displayed the Blue Sun Lord: a cobalt and ebony armored humanoid shape three meters in height, enthroned in the Centari Rampant capital of

Unmoving Glory, surrounded by bionic roses that fluctuated through the visible light spectrum. Celestial power radiated from the Blue Sun, a fraction of the god's true might and omnipotence. Though the god never looked *at* her, she was frozen. Fear, awe, wonder.

"Shhh, child," whispered the woman beside her. "I'm here."

The pilot turned to meet eyes gray like comet dust. The woman squeezed her hand, and for a moment, she forgot she was in the presence of a god.

"Always remember your heart, my dearest."

Hover drones buzzed in and the woman stood. She bent and kissed the side of the pilot's head. The seam of skin and metal faceplate tingled.

"I will always love you."

And then the woman was gone, and the ship was alone, and did not know why it hurt.

I do not remember dreams, she says to Li Sin when her friend wakes from a nap. *What was I like?*

"You were singing, and you were sad."

Li Sin talks to her pilot, but she has become familiar with this; they speak to all of her, for she is the ship.

What was the song? She has disabled her private logs and edited out Li Sin's image and voice from the bridge security feed. She will remember Li Sin, but they will always be a ghost.

Li Sin's face scrunches in a way that makes her think of a person whose face and name she can't recall.

"I think I remember it," Li Sin says. "I can sing for you—"

No, she says, suddenly afraid. *It is not protocol.* The ship is perfect obedience and nothing more.

Ascending Dawn enters Olinara V's planet-space intent on refueling for the journey back to Rigel Prime. Olinara V is a mining colony world, rich in ore and metals. It has grown into a trade station and fueling dock, a nexus between mid-space and the rim of the Principality. Population: seventeen million.

Ascending Dawn likes how Olinara V looks from high orbit: red-gold-gray, speckled with wild cloud formations that dance in the atmosphere to the unheard music of winds.

It's like one of Sigi's paintings, she tells Kosavin.

The first officer smiles, a rare sight. Half her face is locked into an unmoving blue steel mask. "I keep telling Sigi they should sell their landscapes. Sigi's unconvinced their work is worth showing."

I like it, Ascending Dawn says.

"As do I."

Li Sin bursts from hiding while Kosavin is still on the bridge, their eyes wide, hair tangled from sleep. "Dawn, I dreamed something terrible—"

"Who are you?" Kosavin snaps, already scanning Li Sin. "You aren't on my records."

They're a ghost, Ascending Dawn replies to Kosavin's neural implant. *Under my protection.*

Kosavin glares down at the child. "How long have they been here?"

Li Sin steps between the pilot and Kosavin. "Don't be mad at the ship."

The first officer's jaw tightens. The faint hum of her cybernetics and Li Sin's breath are the only sounds on the bridge.

Ascending Dawn's pilot stands and jerkily rests a palm on Li Sin's shoulder. They are the same height. Like the moment when she saw the universe unfold, that undiluted certainty she is part of a living being too vast to comprehend, she knows she can never abandon Li Sin. They are her sibling, the one she knew before her crew, the one she whispers to in secret, the one she values above her protocols.

Li Sin can stay, Ascending Dawn declares, *for they are part of the ship.*

Unexpectedly, Kosavin smiles again. "So this is the anomaly Zeta told me about."

Li Sin glances between Kosavin and Ascending Dawn. "I am?"

Kosavin shrugs. "I've been aware of fluctuations in energy and rations aboard the bridge for some time."

You aren't mad? Ascending Dawn asks.

Kosavin shakes her head. "I was born on a dread-naught seventy standard cycles ago. I know what a threat is and what is not. The child is no danger to the ship."

Li Sin nods, once. Ascending Dawn's pilot feels their trembling with her hand on their shoulder.

"I will schedule a physical for you," Kosavin tells Li Sin. "I'd like Mr. Najem to make sure your health is not compromised."

"I'm supposed to stay hidden," Li Sin whispers.

Kosavin's lip twitches. "I never said it would be on-record, child."

Thank you, Ascending Dawns tells her officer, and Kosavin inclines her head before she leaves the bridge.

Then Ascending Dawn's sensors prickle as she receives direct communication from the Blue Sun Lord's beacons.

BY DECREE OF THE GOLD SUN LORD, OLINARA V IS GUILTY OF HARBORING AN ENEMY OF THE PRINCIPALITY AND WILL BE CLEANSED FROM THE SIGHT OF THE GODS. GLORY UNTO THE SEVEN SUNS, GLORY UNTO THE PRINCIPALITY.

Submessages follow, warning all ships in the system to depart and to initiate no contact with the inhabitants of Olinara V. The world has hidden an escaped slave beholden to the Gold Sun, and no one is to leave the planet. All are rendered traitors and will be punished.

She slows, and her pilot retakes her chair.

Li Sin's face pales and they begin shaking. "Are the gods going to find us?"

No. We will leave the system as ordered.

"But all the people..." Li Sin swallows. "Are they going to die?"

Yes, she says, because she does not have the heart to lie to Li Sin. *It is protocol.*

"I shouldn't have come on board." Li Sin covers their face with both hands. "I'm bad luck."

This is not your fault, Ascending Dawn says, confused at Li Sin's sudden distress.

"I'm always there when bad things happen! I was born on *Moondark Glory Surpassing Time*. And then she died. My family...my other ship..."

What happened?

Tears drip down Li Sin's face. "She died when dust leeches infected the engines."

Dust leeches are noncorporeal entities that drift in the deeper creases of subspace, corrode a ship's matter and destabilize its existence until everything crumbles into dust.

That wasn't your fault. It's a statistical likelihood of traveling in the red-tide subspace routes.

"Moon made me and the ones not infected leave on a shuttle before she—she—"

Self-immolated? Ascending Dawn asks softly, though she knows it must be so. It is a failsafe written into ships that travel red subspace waves. It is said that self-destruction is a mercy.

Li Sin wipes at their face, but they only sob harder. "She's dead. Everyone's dead."

How did you get aboard here? Ascending Dawn asks, wishing she knew how to comfort Li Sin. Her pilot's arms do not feel sufficient to hug her friend.

Li Sin sniffs and blinks against more tears. "I didn't have anywhere to go on Centari Rampant. Then I saw you, and...you sounded so alone. Your doors let me in."

I'm sorry for what happened to you, she says. She is poor substitute for what Li Sin lost.

Li Sin stands up, mouth trembling. "I should go away."

Why?

"I don't want you to be hurt. I don't want anyone else to be hurt because I'm nearby."

But there is nowhere Li Sin might go, except into the void of space.

Stay. Ascending Dawn's pilot slowly reaches out, her hand webbed with implants. *Please? We will be okay. I will protect you.*

She wonders how many of the refugees from Aes August had anyone to tell them the same.

"What about the other people?" Li Sin whispers. "Who will protect them?"

Protocol dictates there is no mercy, no solace, and no hope for those on Olinara V.

She does not like this protocol.

Please report to the bridge, Ascending Dawn texts her officers. To Li Sin, she says, *We will find a way to help.*

Her core officers and Zeta gather on the bridge. Jamil leans close to the viewscreen, as if proximity will give him better insight. All notice Li Sin but after a curt explanation from Kosavin, Li Sin is dismissed as an auxiliary civilian companion to the pilot and they can stay on the bridge.

Everyone has heard the decrees.

"Can we do nothing?" Hayato whispers.

Zeta folds zir legs down until ze kneels beside the pilot's chair. "The efficient course is to obey and leave the system."

"They will all die," Jamil says, his voice numb.

The world will die. Her protocol does not extend to refugees. Even if it did, she cannot save them all. *I wish to know what options we have.*

She feels very small, infinitesimal against the backdrop of the Principality and the might of gods.

Jamil presses his fingertips against the undersides of his eyes. "I know we cannot evacuate an entire planet. But we could save *some* lives. We aren't a warship. We don't have to participate in genocide through inaction."

To break protocol will put the crew in danger.

"I know." He lays a hand against the side of her viewscreen. "We all know."

Illyan Chu, the bi-gender security officer, rubs her beard with a thumb. Her voice is low, rich, and she hides anxiety beneath a calm façade. "I have drones synced to in-ship-only networks. It'll be rough, but I can maintain order in the passenger decks."

Kosavin keeps her spine rigid. "My birthship was a dreadnaught who carried war prisoners for the Violet Sun. Many would be...lost in transit, the ones tagged combatants or enemies who were neither. I have the skill to disable system-based tracking. Our lost prisoners found off-grid lives waiting on rim worlds far from the center of the Principality, but lives nonetheless."

Jamil arches his eyebrows. "Highly illegal, isn't it?"

"Naturally." Kosavin's lip twitches, her microexpression hinting of dark amusement. "It's at your disposal, Mr. Najem."

"We have resources to carry two-thousand non-crew," Sigi adds, their fingers tapping rapidly across a tablet. "If Mr. Najem and Officer Kosavin alter the neural links and disable tracking for Olinara V citizens, we could conceivably evacuate some of the people before the warships decimate the planet's surface. Besides, the warships are under orders from the Gold Sun; they won't notice an empty transport ship from the Blue Sun clearing the sector as ordered."

Kosavin folds her arms behind her back. "Doable," she says. "But we must act now."

Zeta inclines zir head, multi-faceted eyes reflecting the faces of those around zir. "Agreed. Ascending Dawn?"

Everyone waits for her response. She is the ship. Li Sin watches her as intently as her crew. If she violates protocol, if she defies the Sun Lords, she will be hunted for treason. She will no longer be a good ship.

Obedience is not a guilt she can endure. She will not turn away this time.

We will save the ones we can.

One-thousand seven-hundred and five. That is as many people as Sigi can smuggle aboard before Ascending Dawn, fueled while her crew works in frantic haste, must undock and escape the atmosphere before the warships drop from subspace.

Jamil, with aid from his medical staff, modifies neural links while Illyan directs the security drones to shepherd refugees into the appointed bays. Hayato and Zeta commit additional treason by tampering with the Blue Sun Lord's imprint on Ascending Dawn's skin. Her shell is dark, now, muted, so she can no longer hear the will of her god.

It is oddly indifferent to what she has always felt. Has her god not been commanding her all this time?

She disables her automated beacons; she can navigate and coordinate with planetary docks, but she is a shadow to the radar systems of other ships now. Though she cannot hold her breath, the idiom seems appropriate.

She flies away from Olinara V, inputting jump coordinates to subspace routes. She does not look as a hundred honor-guard warships flanking the celestial Gold Sun

Lord drop into orbit around the colony world and begin the bombing.

She mutes all broadcasts escaping Olinara V.

She cannot bear the dying world's screams.

Running dark, Ascending Dawn skirts the outmost fringe of the Principality, unnoticed yet by the Blue Sun Lord. She is not scheduled to return to Rigel Prime for two weeks, and with the disruption—*death*—of Olinara V, Sigi expects they have a buffer of time before the ship's disappearance is logged. Space is vast, Sigi reminds her, and not even the gods can see everything.

Ascending Dawn's skin hums with the desperation and grief of her passengers. But a ship cannot weep.

Kosavin directs her to the rim worlds that are hostile or fractured from the centralized might of the Principality. Kosavin knows well how to make refugees disappear safely into new cities; she can do no more than give the ones they saved a second chance to live. When Ascending Dawn has smuggled everyone taken from Olinara V to a string of rim worlds and asteroid colonies, she is out of time.

In orbit around the fourth moon of Irdor Se, she tells her crew, *You must go now. You are not safe here. Jamil can modify your implants like the others. You can escape.*

There is silence, at first. How can words hurt so much to a ship?

"I cannot leave," Zeta says. "LK-2875 was made for this ship. I would stay, regardless. This is home."

One by one, her each of crew tells her, boldly, quietly, unflinchingly, gladly, that they, too, will stay. They will remain aboard the ship. They are part of *Brightened Star, Ascending Dawn*. She feels as overwhelmed as she did when she saw the universe expand.

But we will be found eventually, she says.

Kosavin nods. "Likely. But not soon."

She looks at them all, on the bridge and at their stations elsewhere: forty-three persons skilled and capable of keeping her running and not alone, who will go into exile with her.

It was my choice to defy the Blue Sun, she says. *I do not want you to be hurt.*

"You didn't do this by yourself," Illyan says. He stretches, grinning. "We chose this lot."

"The Blue Sun will not care." Kosavin tilts her head, a sharp little movement. Her left optic shines with binary code as she sorts data points and probabilities. "And it's done."

Jamil shrugs, the corner of his mouth turned up. "We're staying." His smile widens and he loops his arm about his husband's waist. "It'll be an adventure."

Hayato laughs. "One I would not miss."

Kosavin kneels beside Li Sin. "And you, child?"

"I want to stay with the ship," Li Sin says. "Can I stay, Ascending Dawn?"

Yes.

Kosavin nods, and that is all.

Something swells in Ascending Dawn, rippling through her shipskin and beating in her engines like the heartbeat in her pilot's chest. She will not be left alone in the stars.

Thank you, she tells her family unit.

They disperse to their stations as she calculates the next jump towards Cormorant Sigma and the Arora Nebula System. Kosavin has estimated that it will be a safe harbor for them all until—if—they choose to go elsewhere later.

Will you sing? she asks Li Sin. She wants to give them the memory of her awakening in return; of how she first saw the universe. She will find a way to share it with them. *I'd like to hear my song.*

She is not afraid any more.

Li Sin holds her pilot's hand. They sing to her and now she will remember her song as she glides toward an unknown future.

She finds a glimmer of memory tucked deep inside and allows herself to inspect it at last: that of her mother's eyes and proud smile just for her.

ABOUT THE AUTHORS

Jody Lynn Nye lists her main career activity as 'spoiling cats.' When not engaged upon this worthy occupation, she writes fantasy and science fiction books and short stories. Since 1987 she has published over 40 books and more than 120 short stories. Over the last twenty or so years, Jody has taught in numerous writing workshops and participated on hundreds of panels covering the subjects of writing and being published at science-fiction conventions. She has also spoken in schools and libraries around the north and northwest suburbs. In 2007 she taught fantasy writing at Columbia College Chicago. She also runs the two-day writers workshop at DragonCon. Jody lives in the northwest suburbs of Chicago, with her husband Bill Fawcett, a writer, game designer, military historian and book packager, and a black cat, Jeremy.

When **J.A. Campbell** is not writing she's often out riding horses or working sheep with her dogs. She lives in Colorado with her three cats, her border collies, Kira and Bran, her Traveler, Triska, and her Irish Sailor. She is the author of the Macrow Necromancers series, the Ghost-Hunting Dog series, the Tales of the Travelers, and many other young adult books. She's a member of the Horror Writers Association and the Dog Writers of America Association. She is also the editor for Story Emporium fiction magazine. Find out more at www.writerjacampbell.com.

Sydney Seay is a writer, artist, soon-to-be college student, and the magic user in her D&D campaigns. She lives in Baltimore, Maryland with her family and their spoiled dachshund, where she spends way too much time obsessing over old Sci-Fi television. This is her first published work.

Richard A. Becker has written for micro-budget feature films, encyclopedias, Fortune 500 corporations, radio commercials, roleplaying games and more. His short fiction has been included in anthologies edited by Jay Lake and Nick Mamatas, John L. Thompson and Robert Hood. He is a native of Los Angeles, California.

Gwendolynn Thomas found her voice swapping jokes over the dinner table with her six siblings, learning to be the funny one in the raucous crowd. Now long since moved out to a much quieter home in Cambridge, MA, she's devoted her career to bringing that same humor to the books she writes. You can find her and subscribe to hear about her future works at GwendolynnThomas.com.

Mariah Southworth lives in Northern California. When not writing, she enjoys playing table top role playing games, watching cartoons while curled up with her cat, and reading. Her favorite science fiction writer is Isaac Asimov. She is probably a human.

Alex Pearl is a writer and student in Phoenix, Arizona currently earning his doctorate in Clinical Psychology at Midwestern University. Alex is frequently described as "a stark portrait of exhaustion," "a marvel of aeronautical engineering," and "that boy in the bog that types words." Alex typically writes horror stories, though when the grim grip of The Terrors releases him, he will occasionally tread into the world of wonder and intrigue that is science fiction. Alex lives with his family and their four amazing dogs. The author of two self-published short story collections, this is his first professional publication.

Eneasz Brodski lives in Denver, where he is currently working on his first novel. He fantasizes that if maybe he just yells into the void enough, some day there will be an answer. It's possible he's going about this whole "life" thing the wrong way, but only time will tell. In the meantime, he also produces a biweekly podcast of rationalist fiction at HPMoRpodcast.com, and blogs at DeathIsBadBlog.com.

Marie DesJardin writes both humorous and dramatic speculative fiction, from short stories to novels to screenplays. Credits include Analog Science Fiction and Fact, Compelling Science Fiction, Flash Fiction Online, Helios Quarterly Magazine (featured author), and Story Quest (award winner). By day, Marie produces eLearning for a video surveillance company, which means she never has to ask what anyone else is doing, because she already knows. She has one published SF novel, For the Time Being, and several more in development. Marie resides in Denver, Colorado, travels extensively, and enjoys hiking in the mountains when they're not on fire.

Alex Acks is a writer, geologist, and dapper AF. Their debut novel from Angry Robot Books is Hunger Makes the Wolf. In addition, they've written for Six to Start and been published in Strange Horizons, Lightspeed, Daily Science Fiction, and more. Alex lives in Denver with their two furry little bastards, where they twirl their mustache, watch movies, and bike. For more information, see http://www.alexacks.com.

Amelia Kibbie is a writer, mother, and high school English teacher in a small Iowa town. Amelia's first story, written in the third grade, was a Super Fudge fan fiction. Her major influences as a young reader were Anne Rice and Stephen King, and her love of science fiction began with an addiction to The X-Files. Young Amelia was hardcore Star Wars fan, but in her 30s, she's traitorously switched to Star Trek. She writes short stories and blogs, and is working on four different novels. Her work represents any and every genre from literary to romance to sci-fi to horror. She lives in Iowa City with her husband, baby daughter, a ghost, and three cats who think they own the place. Find more of her work at ameliakibbie. com.

A. Merc Rustad is a queer non-binary writer who lives in the Midwest United States. Favorite things include: robots, dinosaurs, monsters, and tea. Their stories have appeared in Lightspeed, Fireside, Apex, Uncanny, Escape Pod, Shimmer, Cicada, and other fine venues, with reprints included in The Best American Science Fiction and Fantasy 2015, Wilde Stories 2016, Heiress of Russ 2016, and Transcendent 2016. Merc likes to play video games, watch movies, read comics, and wear awesome hats. You can find Merc on Twitter @Merc_Rustad or their website: http://amercrustad.com.

Many many thanks to all of our backers, many of whom chose to be listed here:

RBC & KMC, Mia Kleve, Erin Bradley, Jake Ganor, Sean M. Locke, Peter O'Meara, El sargento Guillermo el soldado colono, Jason Zippay, Benjamin Widmer, E Belzer, Petrov Neutrino, I. W. Nettleship, Christopher Flint, Peter Sartucci, Jonathan Wager, Melissa Honig, Shawn Scarber, Sheryl R. Hayes, Adam Zimpfer, Terry Tuttle, Andrea Brummund, Ade Hirsch, Mary Ratliff, Todd Zircher, Olivia Isaacs, Lachlan Bakker, Jonathan Miller, Christina Rowe, Charles Warrington, Bernd Wolff, Preston Poland, Cassie T, Henry De Sarno, omnibrain, Marcus Walker, Lee Ann Rucker, Meeghan C. Appleman, Andrew Topperwien, James Loopstra, Anja Carl, Thomas M. Colwell, Rico Gilbert, William H Rabe III, Simo Muinonen, Robert SPL Chatterjee, Tjerk van den Bos, Ehud Kaminer, Rowland allsopp, Alby Darling, Eric Cargal, C Gilchrist, Raena King, Zeno, David Meilhac, Cynthia Gonsalves, Jorden Varjassy, James Lucas, Kristina, William Randol, Leewelo Lorekeeper, Margaret St. John, Kai Nikulainen, Devan Rhinehart, Hannah Lesnik, Matthew Hieb, Peter 'Malkira' Lennox, JKB, David and Sayaka Wright, Rachelle R., DaveS Trainer to the Stars, Judy Kashman, Elizabeth Creegan, Nick W, Ari Baronofsky, Natalie S., James 'Apollo' Hancock, Brooke Orosz, Mark Urbin, Steven "Sweyn" Seyler, CuDunn, Joe Wiggins, Andrew Jones, Kathryn "Cho" Yee, Ayame Suzaku, Rhiannon Raphael, Ifer (xeno-bio-sociology & ihasafandom), Wanda Sissle, Jesse S. Williams, Tomas Burgos-Caez, David Starkey, Fred Herman, O. Westin, A. C. Smingleigh, Sune Bøegh, Jared Goerner, Kristin Luna, Lydia Trethewey, Josh King, Sarah Urfer, Carol A. Jones, V. Hartman DiSanto, E. Morningstar, Lenn, Melissa Dora Colbeth, Chad Bowden, Chris 'Warcabbit' Hare, Kerry aka Trouble, Bridget, Ro, Jessica Enfante, Kim Jenkinson, jose n, Kelsi Parker, Ross Hathaway, Douglas 'Argowal' Reid, RKBookman, Aggie Ninepence, Revek,

Lisa Barmby-Spence, House Fretful, Keith Bissett, Claire Rosser, Laurie Hicks, Smashingsuns, Louise McCulloch, -Grey Jones, David E Mumaw, Mike Maurer, A Goad, Full-time Medic; part-time Human, Bennett Jackson, Nicole McPherson, James Williams, Jonah Sutton-Morse, Paul A. and Rebecca J. Verlinden, Gacel, Derek J. Jackson, Dave Bush, Marie Blanchet, Mary Kay Kare, Laura Murray, Jay Kominek, Isaac 'Will It Work' Dansicker, Marc Hartstein, Travis Heermann, Michelle Six, Meredith Buckley, Alex Christensen, Matthew Blackwell, [NAME REDACTED], Judy Waidlich, Jef Lay, Stacy Fluegge, Simon Callan, Frank Nissen, Thomas Smith, Joshua Gerdes, Katharyn Elin Garcia, David Starner, Gustaf B., Nathan Barra, Matt Eyre, Erika Altman, Danielle Ackley-McPhail, Lydia Eickstaedt, Alain Fournier, Joy Dawn Johnson, Mat Masding-Grouse, Annelies, Jakub Narębski, Sam Knight, Colin Lloyd, Thomas A. Fowler, Michael Carson, Tyler Taute, Angela Carlson, Benjamin Hausman, Alan Danziger, Miles P Cusick, Svend Andersen, Mike "Lazarus" Henthorne, Amy Chused, Dave Heyman, Nathan Turner, Jake and Beverly Coutts, Stephanie Lucas, Celeste Joiner, Cubbage/Kannarr family, Robin Reed, Raymond Finch, James B. Joiner, David Mortman, William Hughes, Scott Schaper, Aramanth Dawe, Stephen Cheng, Max Kaehn, Eric-Christian Koch, Ben Sinclair, Ryan Harris, Astlyr, Rocky Williams, John Carroll, Jeffrey Andres Williams, Elizabeth Selby, D. Wes Rist, Amy Dobbins, Katrina "katster" Templeton, Matt McCoy, Y. H. Lee, Karl K. Gallagher, Oliver Cole, H Grunefeld, Jeanne Kramer-Smyth, Bethan Thomas, NoSmokey Bear, Katy Phelan, Jeremy Frost, Katherine Malloy, David Howansky, W. Switsers, stevie, Shervyn, Ivan Donati, Leigh, John D. Payne, Lucie Le Roux, Caitlin Jane Hughes, Helen Savore, April Steenburgh, Emy Peters, Arianna J. Howard, Quentin Lancelot Fagan, Bill Gimbel, Kato Thompson, Benjamin Howarth, M.C.A. Hogarth, and Anna Glauser.

ABOUT THE EDITOR

When not fighting crime or tinkering with Tarot spreads, Vivian Caethe writes weird fiction, science fiction, fantasy, quirky nonfiction and everything in between. She has an MFA in Creative Writing from Regis University that she finds useful as a wall decoration. She lives in Colorado with her super genius cat and can be found as a writer at http://www.viviancaethe.com and as an editor at http://wordsmadebeautiful.net.

84716519R00133

Made in the USA
San Bernardino, CA
10 August 2018